It's A Wonderful Death

E. N. McMAHON

Published by Nick de Blegny Publishing

ISBN: 0615922058

ISBN-13: 9780615922058

DEDICATION

To Kevin, without whom nothing in my life is complete

DEDICATION

To Kevin, without whom nothing in my life is complete

ACKNOWLEDGMENTS

This book could not have been written without the constant support, insight, and encouragement of Kevin Rattan. Special thanks to Philip Spitzer of The Spitzer Literary Agency, Lukas Ortiz, and Luc Hunt.

Thanks to Matt Smith for his atmospheric cover. Other examples of his work can be found at www.shimuzu.co.uk.

CHAPTER ONE

George Bailey lived at 320 Sycamore. Like a lot of the houses on this street in Bedford Falls, it was gothic Victorian - four stories high, with enough gables and pointed turrets for you to wonder if some damsel in distress was languishing inside, lurking by a high window and waiting for the right moment to let down her golden hair. I was no knight in shining armor, but I approached anyway, picking my way through the snowdrifts along the pathway. My hat was slanted low, and my coat buttoned high. My hair was combed, and my suit was pressed with a crease sharp enough to cut your pinky on. I wore an expression of concern and circumspection for all the world to see. I looked the way a detective brought in from the Albany DA's office ought to look when he was about to serve a warrant.

The place was lit up like an ocean liner. The front door was open, and there was no one to stop me going in. An oversized heap of Christmas tree, done up in gold and silver, took up the far corner of the sitting room. The tree made me think of a big-boned homely girl decked out in her best get-up: no prize looker, but the effort taken was apparent.

From the center of the room rose a steep oaken

staircase. The steps were battered with use, and a couple of the banisters were broken. At the foot of the stairs, a man with watery amber eyes and a taffy-colored moustache loitered, slouch-shouldered. A box Brownie was balanced against his shin. As soon as he noticed me, he snapped to attention. "You that fella from the DA's office?"

"Yes."

He pulled out a notepad and pencil. "What's the word on Bailey?"

I gave him a cold eye. "No comment."

A small balding man with black-rimmed glasses sat on the bottom step. He glanced up at me. "Name's Carter," he said. "Bank examiner. I was hoping to spend Christmas with my family." His glasses magnified his eyes and he stared at me a moment, accusingly. "In Elmira." Then he looked ahead, resolutely, at nothing.

We were the three wise men, waiting at the bottom of Bailey's staircase. The minutes trudged by like an army in full retreat. I took out my pint of old Napoleon and downed a swig. Carter looked up at me, his eyes behind the lenses as large as a lizard's. I offered him the bottle, but he shuddered and looked away.

I held the bottle out to the newsman. "May as well share some Christmas cheer."

The newsman laughed, and reached for the bottle. "Thanks mister. My name's Eddie Turner. From the Herald-Traveler."

"I'm Richard Incles," I said. "I-N-C —"

But Turner had already put his pencil away. He took a nip, winked, and took another. He handed the bottle back. "What a way to spend a Christmas Eve." He wiped his mouth with the back of his hand. "Old man Potter got to your boss too, huh?"

I nodded. A nod can't be quoted.

"Called my editor and told him George Bailey was going down and it was the biggest story this county has ever seen." Turner shrugged. "So here I am."

"It must be swell to be the richest man in town, and call all the shots."

"Potter's got a lot of pull," Turner said. "That nobody can deny."

"Except he's no jolly good fellow."

Turner snorted, and reached down to fiddle with his camera. "You got that right."

I took another nip, and was slipping the bottle back into my pocket when the door rattled in a fresh gust of wind. A tall skinny rake of a man, with a freshly busted lip and glittering, glassy black eyes, rushed in. I recognized him, from just a half-hour ago, when I'd been waiting in Potter's office. Grinning like a maniac, he'd rapped on Potter's window, shouted out a Merry Christmas, and galloped onwards into the dark and snowy street. Now he was just grinning like a maniac.

"Mary!" he called out. Then he took notice of us three, each in turn. His grin got wider, and the gleam in his eye more intense. "Well, hello Mr. Bank Examiner!"

Carter stood up. George Bailey grabbed Carter's hand, and shook it. He was drunk, or crazy, or something worse. But I'd seen meaner faces that night, on some of the town's finest citizens.

"Mr. Bailey, there's a deficit," Carter said.

"I know!" George Bailey said. "About eight thousand dollars."

I reached into my coat. "I have a little paper here."

"I bet it's a warrant for my arrest. Isn't it wonderful!"

Turner scooped up his camera and snagged a shot.

"Mary!" Bailey called out again. He ran up the stairs, and at the second floor landing, three or four kids in pajamas emerged from their bedrooms and trooped around him. "Kids!" he said. "Mary - Ma-"

A woman with light brown hair the color of honey catching the sunlight rushed over the front door threshold. She was a little out of breath. She was the kind of woman a man could look forward to coming home to, a nice face that got nicer the more you looked at it. It was the kind of face that made you think of holding hands and running shoeless through the summer grass, if you were the hand-holding, running-shoeless-in-the-summer-grass type, that is. I wasn't. But I was also willing to bet that if the wolf ever came to her door, she wouldn't be any Little Red Riding Hood about it.

She glanced at me, and gave a distracted smile as she hurried into the sitting room. She took hold of a side table, and with a single movement, swept everything on it to the floor. "It's a miracle, George," she said.

Carter of Elmira cleared his throat with a dry rasping cough, and opened his mouth to speak. The front door banged, and a fresh gust of wind swept over us.

A befuddled-looking old codger, chubby as an overgrown infant, bustled in, followed by a couple of dozen townspeople. The old man had wire-framed glasses and he wore a summer straw hat perched way back on his head. In front of his pot belly, he carried a laundry basket overflowing with greenbacks and coins.

"Come in, Uncle Billy," Mrs. Bailey said. "Everybody! In here!"

"Mary did it, George!" the codger said. "They didn't ask any questions - just said: 'George is in trouble -'"

I renewed my acquaintance with Napoleon. The whole town, except for Potter, came sweeping over the threshold like a human snowstorm.

A swarthy-faced man in late middle age stepped forward. In his spindly arms he cradled a mixing bowl filled to the brim with cash. He was tidy and spare and wore an old-fashioned silk waistcoat under his suit coat.

"I busted the juke-box, too," he said. He had an Italian accent.

"Mr. Martini!" someone called out. "Merry Christmas."

A large cored woman entered, digging money out of a long black stocking. A substantial-looking, fat-faced citizen emptied his wallet into the basket. Then he pulled out his pocket watch, smiled and gave it to the little girl in George Bailey's arms.

"And here's something for you to play with," the man said.

An old gent stepped up, a large glass jar full of notes and coins cradled under his arm. He was spry as a grasshopper, and almost dainty in his movements. He had a woolen scarf folded neatly around his neck. He looked modest, dignified and respectable, but you could tell from the flush of veins crisscrossing his nose, he'd enjoyed a drink now and again. With a rustle and a rattle, he emptied the jar into the basket. He gave a discrete smile to George, and stepped aside.

"Mr.Gower!" George said.

With a shock wave of scent to announce her, a woman approached. She was a dame if there ever was one. She had blond hair bright as a neon sign, and a fine full length of leg. It was the kind of leg that went on like a tone poem, with plenty of swell and no unwelcome sharps.

"Violet Bick," George said. It was as though the characters from a much-loved book were springing to life before his eyes, and like a child, he identified each one out loud. And I recognized that name. Potter had told me that George Bailey was slipping Violet Bick money on the sly. I could see there were a lot of reasons why, some blond, some long, and some rounded, but all good.

"I'm not going to go, George," Violet Bick said. "I've changed my mind." She dropped a pretty sum onto the table. I opened my bottle and took another visit to St Helena. Violet Bick could have come with me if she wanted.

No such luck. Instead, the townspeople burst into a chorus of "Hark the Herald Angels Sing." I took a swig of my own brand of Christmas spirit. At the end of the carol, they cheered and applauded. A shush went up, and Mary Bailey read a telegram aloud. A fellow named Sam Wainwright advanced Bailey up to $25,000, stop, hee-haw and Merry Christmas. As Mary and George Bailey hugged, a young man in a Naval Commander's uniform barreled through the open door. A thickset, ginger-haired cop was at his side. The young man had a smooth, complacent brow, and a nice lot of metal pinned to his chest. He took a glass of wine and held it aloft for a toast.

"To my big brother George," he said. "The richest man in town."

Carter sighed. He dug into his pocket, and with a defeated shrug, tossed a few bills onto the pile. I looked at the warrant in my hands. With all the cash flying through the air and landing in a nice tidy bundle in Mrs. Bailey's front room, it was as though no money had ever gone missing. I knew Mooney would tell me to stick to the point, that the first eight thousand dollars was still unaccounted for. But Potter seemed to be the only one who would care, and now, what could he prove? I would go back to Potter and tell him the money had simply been misplaced and it had since been found. If Mooney or Potter didn't like it, they could go hang.

I caught Violet Bick's eye and she smiled. I stepped up to the table, ripped the warrant in two, and joined in a loud chorus of Auld Lang Syne. I had another drink or three, and after that, the party began to break up.

Mrs. Bailey stood by the door. "Good-bye, and thank you!" she said. She looked around, and then said, as if to herself, "Now where has George gone to?" She was still scanning the room when one of the kids began pulling at her skirt.

"Tommy, say 'thank you' to all daddy's friends," she said.

Tipping my hat goodbye, I went out of the claustrophobic warmth into the cold white streets, where the snow was as pure as a debutante's reputation, and as slated for sullying. I got in my car and headed back to Potter's. I was turning the corner onto Washington Street when I had to slam on the brakes. It was either that or run smack into some chump who was crossing the street and memorizing the cracks in the pavement instead of watching the traffic.

It was Mr. Gower. He was still the picture of respectability, from mid-distance, but he was muttering to himself. I rolled down the window.

"You okay, Mr. Gower?"

He tottered up to my car. "As well as anybody can be after having to deal with that man." He gestured in the direction of the bank. "I would have stayed longer at the Baileys, but Potter called me and demanded that I - well, I delivered his order alright." He looked at me, and he remembered to smile. "A promise is a promise. And after all, it is Christmas." He continued on his way.

The light in Potter's office was still on. It was almost twenty-five past. I parked, went up to the door, and knocked, for the second time that night. This time, I was about to get chewed out for destroying a warrant. But I'd done worse in my time. And Potter and my boss could both do with reminding that the services of DA's office were not for sale, or even for rent. Or at least, they shouldn't be.

Potter's yellow-faced henchman opened the door.

"I need to speak to Mr. Potter, please."

The goon's nostrils located me in the dark distance beneath him. Without a word, he ushered me in.

CHAPTER TWO

Potter was sitting at his desk as though he hadn't moved since I left him. His account book was open in front of him. He glanced up with irritation, and then seeing it was me, smiled sickly-sweetly, as if I was a nice guy and shooting the breeze with me was the greatest pleasure anyone could have on a Christmas Eve. The smile came to him about as naturally as tap-dancing to a tarantula.

"Back so soon, my boy?" He put his pen down and clasped his hands, mild as schoolboy saying grace. Then he experimented with another smile, broader, and more conspiratorial than sweet. The experiment failed. "And what has happened with our friend George Bailey?"

"Bailey's at home with his wife and kids," I said. "That's where he'll be staying, too. Until he goes back to work the day after tomorrow at the Building and Loan. The investigation is over."

"Over!"

"Finished. Complete. Terminated. If you hand me that thesaurus over there, I'll give you some other choices. The meaning will be the same, and I think you understand it."

"You miserable lit-" Potter began. His voice broke into a raspy, sputtering cough. From the left pocket of his waistcoat, he extracted a pill, put it in his mouth, and swallowed. The coughing subsided. "Give me that warrant." He reached out and his hand flapped open in front of my chest like a hungry Venus fly trap. "I'll see it gets served."

"Can't," I said. "I've ripped it in two. It seems the money was misplaced, and now it's been found. I just wanted you to know. To put the mind of a good citizen at rest. Oh, and Merry Christmas."

Potter picked up the phone receiver and began to dial. "Just wait a minute, my boy. I have something for you." Then he growled into the phone. "Mooney? I want Mooney. I don't care if your father is busy, you get him on the phone now... Mooney, Potter. I have some business I want seen to immediately. It seems your errand boy has taken matters into his own hands. He's destroyed the warrant. Yes. That's right." Potter's voice went silky with insinuation. "Now, you can't tolerate such insubordination, can you? I think you'll have to do something, don't you? Yes, he's right here. I'll pass the phone over to him. Be glad to."

I took the receiver. "I destroyed the warrant, Mooney. The cash has been returned, all eight thousand dollars."

Mooney sputtered into the line. "You can't just go around destroying warrants. You're supposed to follow procedure."

"Procedure's just a tired lawman's way of saying he doesn't have a clue what to do."

"You won't be any kind of lawman after this stunt."

"If you want to fire me, okay. I can always make a go of it as a private eye."

"Have you been dipping into those fool detective novels again?" He didn't sound like he wanted me to answer. "Try living in the real world, why don't you? It'll be an adjustment but you might find you like it."

Potter watched me with his glittering green-black eyes. I studied him as Mooney went on cataloguing my faults.

I'd heard them all before but I managed not to yawn. Potter's eyebrows were black, composed of many fine lines, like an etching. His mouth was a single straight line that you could imagine saying "no" a lot. He looked like he belonged on the back of some especially cold, hard currency.

"Incles, you know this isn't the first time you've messed up," Mooney said. "You charged that woman in Rowley with running a morphine ring. Turned out she was a diabetic who took insulin. You remember. The police chief's sister."

"Her garbage was full of little brown bottles. With her brother being who he was, she wouldn't even have had to buy protection. It was the perfect set-up. So I got suspicious. And any cop worth his salt would have too."

"Then there was the time you hauled in old man Bartlett for kidnapping. Wound up that a couple of his grandchildren were visiting from Albuquerque. False arrest. He's still threatening to sue."

"No one in the neighborhood had seen those kids before. It smelled funny, that's all. So maybe Bartlett was no kidnapper - that time. But I still wonder what he's got cooking behind that picket fence and the honeysuckle."

There was a long pause. "You're like that guy in the story, tilting at windmills," Mooney said. "You see what isn't there. I'm supposed to be your boss, not some darn sidekick cleaning up the messes you make." He took a deep breath, and released it. "I've covered for you as long as I can, but I can't fight Potter. You're out. Not just this case, Incles. Forever."

"Merry Chris-" I began.

Mooney had already rung off. Those were the only chimes I'd heard all Christmas. But they'd given me my wings, and I was free to fly.

Potter snatched the receiver from me, and hung up the phone. "Go on now. See if George Bailey can help you out." He gave a laugh as short and dry as a midget crossing the Mojave in the company of Mormons.

"Merry Christmas, Mr. Potter."

"And a happy New Year to you - in the poorhouse." Potter chuckled and turned back to his accounts. The only sound was his pen scratching across the page, and then the door closing as I let myself out.

CHAPTER THREE

I walked through the snowy silent streets to my car. I was minus a job. But I had a fresh pint of rye waiting for me in my room. I decided to head back to the boarding house on Central. On my way, I passed by a bar, Martini's. I pulled over. No cutesy lettering on the sign, or fake antique spelling, or ladies night specials advertised. I'd seen this kind of bar before. It was the kind that served hard liquor to men who wanted to get drunk fast, and that suited me fine.

The front room was as crowded as a turkey pen the day after Thanksgiving. But from a table in the back, a chorus of singing rose. A dark-browed beefcake of a man stood behind the bar. He was rolling up his sleeves. Then he grabbed a dish cloth, and started polishing the same spot of wood over and over, as if he was brooding over it. He looked up at me and kept at it.

"Scotch," I said. "Double."

"Sure thing, bub." He tossed the cloth over his shoulder, poured a glass of scotch, and set it down in front of me.

I reached into my pocket and drew out my wallet. All I had three dimes and a fuzzy cough drop. Not enough by a long shot.

"Do I pay for it now?" I said.

The barman's face went stiff. He planted his hands flat in front of him on the bar and drew himself up. He was well-muscled, glowering, and mean, the type that tends to gain weight in captivity. He had an arrogant strength to him, like something waiting to pounce, that I bet came in handy in this town of two-bit chiselers and grim-faced henchmen. His jaw was locked into a permanent expression of belligerence, and his nose was flattened sideways against his face, like a door left ajar.

"That's the usual system. Unless you got some better idea."

I checked my inside coat pocket, and came up empty. I was practically withering under the barman's charm when an old man stepped behind the bar. It was Martini himself.

"What's the problem, my friend?" Martini said. "You forget your wallet?"

"Or something like that," the barman said. He glowered and made a fist.

"Nick, you take it easy," Martini said. "Just back from break and already you making trouble. On Christmas Eve! This man helped George Bailey. He tore the warrant up into confetti." Martini smiled and patted me on the shoulder. "You forget the warrant, my friend, we forget the bill." He gave Nick a look and moved on. The barman frowned, and lurched off to rub out some fresh patch of bar.

I drank slowly at first. That was okay. Then I washed the whole thing down in a hurry. That was better, for a moment. I was on my feet and struggling to get my arms through the sleeves of my coat when I felt a hand on my shoulder.

This hand was not as friendly as Mr. Martini's. Nor did I feel its owner was about to buy me a drink.

"Are you Richard Incles, from the DA's office?"

I turned and faced a broad-faced bumbler of a cop. I had seen him at Bailey's house. He was a mere snow blossom of about one hundred and ninety-eight pounds, with a chest as deep as a walk-in freezer. He was stern, slow and deliberate. You could imagine him digesting a single thought as though it were an entire Christmas dinner.

"That's half right," I said. "I'm Incles, but as of a quarter hour or so, I'm no longer from the DA's office. Get it?"

He thought it over. "Wise guy," he said. "You're coming with me. You're wanted for questioning. In connection with murder."

CHAPTER FOUR

I could tell he didn't have much practice with this procedure. I kicked the bar stool back and stood up. My gun nearly fell out of my shoulder holster, but the man in blue was oblivious. He took out a pair of handcuffs, and regarded them ruefully.

"Aw, doggone it," he said. "Let's skip it. We're not going far."

"Whose murder?"

"If you don't know already, you'll find out soon enough. Maybe I shouldn't even have told you that much."

I held my hand out. "As you know, I'm Incles. Ex-DA. And you are -"

"Bert," he said. His face cracked into a smile so broad it was like watching a big slice getting taken out of a pumpkin pie. He started to reach his hand out. Then he remembered. "Okay, pal, that's enough." The slice of pie went back.

He held me by my left elbow and directed me along the street. It was still snowing, but up ahead, I could see there was some commotion at the corner by the Savings and Trust. The door was open and light streamed onto the dark street. Two police cars were parked outside.

"Is it Potter?"

"Let's just say it isn't Santa Claus," Bert said. "And don't tell anybody I told you that either."

The snow crunched under our feet. We were almost within range of the yellow rectangle of light cast by the bank's windows.

"Just tell the truth, son, and you'll be alright. A lot better than if you don't."

"That used to be my line."

Bert laughed. He stiff-armed me through the open door, and led me quickly past Potter's office. I glanced into it.

Someone had gone to a lot of trouble to stuff a special Christmas turkey. Henry Potter was sitting behind his desk, same as before, except his mouth was open and he was facing the ceiling. A few fistfuls of greenbacks were stuffed down his gullet.

He was dead.

CHAPTER FIVE

Callaghan conducted the questioning. He was a youngster with a blanched, stricken-eagle look to his face. I guessed he was still in his late twenties, but already his hair had gone completely white, probably in a single night, over some jaywalking case he couldn't crack. He had pale blue eyes, cold as pond ice, and keen as a knife point. His build was skinny, and his gray suit swallowed him up like a light-weight gabardine whale.

Callaghan had set up shop in Potter's back room. He didn't expect me to be brought in so soon. He had a plate of spaghetti in front of him. Bert propelled me forward by my left elbow. Callaghan looked up from his plate. He pushed it guiltily aside. He picked up a paper napkin and daubed at his thin colorless lips.

"Here he is, boss." Bert pushed his hat back a few inches and rubbed his brow.

"Okay," Callaghan said. "Good work, officer. I'd like you to wait outside a moment."

Bert nodded, and lumbered into the hallway.

Callaghan had a blank sheet of paper in front of him. "Incles, from the DA's?" He began doodling on the sheet as he spoke.

"I used to be. From the DA's office that is. I'm still Incles. Same as this morning."

"Did you speak to Henry Potter at this office earlier tonight?" He was in the middle of a figure-eight design.

"Yes. Mooney called me down here around ten tonight, as you already know. I arrived at Potter's office around eleven."

"The first time. Then you went to George Bailey's house, on Sycamore, at which point you failed to serve the warrant for his arrest. At eleven-thirty or so, you came back here, Mr. Potter called Mooney, and you were fired." Callaghan's figure-eight was growing in complexity to a figure eight hundred and eighty eight.

"You know the story," I said.

He set down his pen. "And is that when you killed Henry Potter?"

"No. I didn't kill him, then or any other time."

"I'm sure Bedford Falls is crawling with homicidal murderers." Callaghan was too young and thin to be sarcastic. On him, a sarcastic smile just looked sour and wan.

"As opposed to murderers who aren't homicidal." I was enjoying watching a young gray police detective get strung up by words that floated past him, menacing but indistinct, like suspects on a shadowy street.

He gave me a pale blue glare. "Just watch it, pal. We may be seeing a lot of each other."

"How's that?"

"For years, people here hated Henry Potter, but nobody touched him. Now, the first and only night you come to town, he gets you fired and within the hour, he's dead. Any comment you'd like to make?" He started a new doodle. This one was based on a tic-tac-toe grid.

"I didn't know Potter enough to hate him that much," I said. "He called the DA's office because he wanted to get Bailey. I just happened to be the lucky fellow Mooney sent along."

"Potter's personal assistant, Mr. Whittier, told us that you had a blow-up with Potter. Can you tell us about that?" Suddenly he wasn't a "me" anymore. He was an "us." It happens to all the brass sooner or later.

"Sure. Potter wanted to lower the boom on Bailey. Eight thousand dollars was discovered missing from the Building and Loan. Potter called for a warrant for Bailey's arrest. I went to Bailey's house to serve the warrant, and concluded that the money had been misplaced and was now restored. So I destroyed the warrant, and Potter blew a gasket. By the way, where was Sunshine Whittier during all of this?"

"I'll ask the questions, Mr. Incles. Potter wanted to locate the whereabouts of the money, you say." He stopped doodling and looked at me. There was a faint ring of tomato sauce about his mouth.

"No, I wouldn't say that. Potter was interested in something else entirely. He told me he'd make sure Bailey was run out of town for good."

Callaghan pulled a ledger book over to him and opened it. Potter's copperplate handwriting filled the page. He had a clear script, and even upside down I could make out the final entry: "December 24, $8000." That was an interesting coincidence.

"Have you ever seen George Bailey?"

"At his home, 320 Sycamore."

"No place else?"

"A little earlier, when I was at Potter's office, I saw a man outside, running by on the street. He stopped, rapped on Potter's window and wished him a Merry Christmas. Later I found out that man was George Bailey."

"How did he seem to you when you saw him by the window?"

"Drunk, or dazed, but almost elated."

"And then, when you saw him at his home?"

"Pretty much the same."

"Before you left, what did Bailey say to you?"

"Nothing. He wasn't there when I left."

Callaghan stopped doodling and locked eyes with me. "So he slipped out. And the whole evening he seemed strange, almost elated you said." He drew a line through his latest effort, like a skewer. "As though maybe he knew he would finally be free."

"Hold on. I didn't say that."

"No. You've done a lot better than that. You're released, Incles, for now. You're in luck - Potter's assistant swears he saw Potter alive after you left. But don't try to skip town. We may want you later on."

He called in a deputy. "We've established a motive. We've located him in the vicinity of Potter's office earlier tonight, and later on he slipped out by himself. And we know he was acting strangely all night."

Callaghan reached over for his plate of spaghetti. By now, it was about as appetizing as stone-cold pasta eaten next door to a room with a stiffening corpse ever can be.

"Make out a warrant for the arrest of George Bailey," he said. "We're looking at murder one."

CHAPTER SIX

I drove back to the boarding house on Central, and parked right smack in front of it, as if I owned the place.

Mrs. Parker ran the boarding house. You would not think of calling Mrs. Parker "Ma." Even in best of circumstances, like, say, you were her child, which maybe on second thought, wouldn't be the best of circumstances. Mrs. Parker had eyes cold and black like the dregs of last night's coffee. Her thin dark hair was drawn back so tightly that her eyebrows were lifted in an expression of perpetually satisfied suspicion. She also pinch-hit for the operator of the town's small switchboard and maybe she knew a few things she shouldn't. She unfailingly wore a sweater and draped at least one afghan about her shoulders. She pulled them tighter when she spoke to you, as if the enduring chill of your presence might soon find itself endured no longer. Mrs. Parker was no Mrs. Santa Claus. But she had a room for rent when I needed one.

I searched my pockets. I still had the three dimes and the fuzzy cough drop. I had forgotten my key. I sprinted up the front steps and knocked at the door. The house was dark. A light went on in the second floor, and then down the hallway to the door. I could see a figure through the frosted glass coming closer, clutching her sweater tighter around her throat.

She drew the curtain back from the door. Her eyes peered at me. With a metallic thud, the lock was unlatched. The door flung open.

"Jesus, Mary and Joseph!" she said. "If I haven't got enough to do, young man. You're lucky I'm still here – I'd be at my niece's this minute but for the snow." She pointed her chin in the direction of a hand-lettered sign above the mantelpiece: "Management requests paying guests retire to their rooms by 8 pm for the evening."

"I imagine you've had quite a night," she said.

I wondered how much she knew. I figured she heard Potter talk to Mooney and then Mooney talk to me. I wondered if she knew about Potter yet.

"Mrs. Parker - ma'am," I said. I liked the official respectful sound of that "ma'am." "I'll be staying here indefinitely, at the request of the DA."

Her face brightened up, and in an instant, slumped down. "But what about the rent? I heard it with my own two ears. You've been fi-" Then she went silent.

I'd pondered that problem myself, but wasn't going to let on. "I'm here on official police business." True enough. No need to say which side of the law I was on this time. I nodded gravely. "You understand."

I could tell she did not. But she said nothing, just gripped the neck of her sweater a little closer and chewed her lips. She nodded, silent as a red Indian, and opened the door to the staircase that led up to my room.

As I was opening my door, she called up the dark stairwell. "Terrible thing about Mr. Potter. And George Bailey arrested for it too!"

CHAPTER SEVEN

I had just closed my eyes, it felt like, when I was woken by a rapid fire knocking on my door. Dim gray light was beginning to seep through the flimsy curtains. I heard a few cars passing on the road below and every now and then the scrape of a shovel on the pavement.

I struggled to get my arms through my shirt sleeves and then I opened the door.

Mrs. Parker stood there. She had a sprig of holly pinned at her collar. She sucked in her breath. She was not pleased, but she was the kind who was pleased to be not pleased.

"Mr. Incles, a call for you just came in." She held up a small folded piece of paper. "I took a message. This is the first and last time I intend to do such a thing. I am a telephone operator, not a personal answering service. The sooner you understand that, the better."

"Thanks, Mrs. Parker," I said. "Merry Christmas."

"Don't get smart, young man," she said. "I'll be at my niece's for the day. I will not be back until evening." She turned to go down the stairs. She looked back at me. "Oh. A Merry Christmas to you too."

I closed the door and opened the note. It read: "Mr.

Incles - Mrs. Bailey wants to see you immediately. IMPORTANT." Mrs. Parker had a tiny scrawl, like the print of mice feet across the bottom of a sink, but for the last word, she'd made an exception.

I figured I had nothing to lose. Trouble had followed me as sure as Christmas Day follows Christmas Eve. It had hung a stocking over the mantelpiece with my name embroidered across it, and it was time to rush down the stairs and open the contents.

I drove over to 320 Sycamore. This time, only a few lights were on and the front door was shut. I knocked on the door and looked at myself in the brass plate. I had looked better on other mornings, in other brass plates.

Mrs. Bailey answered the door. She tried to smile. She had on a simple navy blue dress with lace collar and cuffs. Her shoes were a shade too stylish to be called sensible but no showgirl would have been caught dead in them either.

She led me inside. The children were playing quietly under the tree. An older, well-dressed woman sat beside them in a faded armchair. She had her feet planted on the floor in front of her and looked steadily ahead at nothing.

"Mr. Incles, this is my mother, Mrs. Hatch. Mother, this is Mr. Incles. He's going to help George out of the fix he's in. Excuse me a minute, Mr. Incles." She raised her voice. "Children, let's scoot into the kitchen and make those gingerbread men. I'll get you started."

One by one, the brats stood up. There were four of them. The older boy wore a crumpled pirate's hat made of construction paper. It came down over his left eye and he bumped into a bookshelf on his way to the kitchen. At the threshold, he turned and stuck his tongue out at me. Then he shut the door behind him.

The old woman looked up. She gazed steadily into my face. Her eyes were sad. "I certainly hope you are capable, Mr. Incles. If anything went wrong, I could not go on." She hesitated and looked down at her hands. "Too many men in this family have met with misfortune. George's passing."

"Hold on, Mrs. Hatch," I said. "George is in jail, that's true, but they've hardly strapped him in the chair just yet."

She winced. Then her face took on a far-away look and her voice softened and slowed and sounded distant too, as if it were coming not just from a different place inside of her but from a different time. "I didn't mean Mary's George, Mr. Incles. I meant my own husband." She twisted her wedding ring. "It will be two years ago this February." She steadied her chin, looked out the window, and forgot I was there.

Mrs. Bailey came back into the room, and glanced at her mother with a worried frown. "The children could use your help in there, mother."

"Of course, you'll want to talk to Mr. Incles alone," Mrs. Hatch said. She may have been day-dreaming but she knew the score. She rose to her feet, and straightened her dress. It was a rich maroon material, simply cut. She checked her earrings. They were fat pearl buttons nestled in heavy gold, and clicked like loose teeth. She gave me a barely perceptible nod as she left the room.

Mrs. Bailey sat down. "Thank you for coming, Mr. Incles, on such short notice, and on Christmas Day. Your family must miss you." It wasn't my family she was thinking of. Her eyes were tearing up. But I knew she wouldn't let those tears fall, not in front of me. She was a lady, I had to admit.

"George - Mr. Potter-" She clasped her hands and tried again. "George has been arrested for the murder of Mr. Potter. I know he didn't do it." She straightened the lace doily on the sofa arm, and looked at me. "We need you to help us, Mr. Incles."

"Mrs. Bailey, the DA's office sent me to Bedford Falls to arrest your husband," I said. "What makes you think I could help him?" This was a fumble down a dark hallway to see how far Mrs. Parker's phone line extended.

Mrs. Bailey fingered the edge of her cuff and looked at

me, dead level. "I'd heard you'd set up as a private investigator."

"Unofficially, yes," I said. "I see Mrs. Parker had a busy Christmas Eve."

"Since you're available, Mr. Incles. You don't know what it means to me, to my family. You've got to help us prove George is innocent."

I figured I had a part in getting him arrested, not the best start to being a private investigator. But I liked the idea of poking the authorities in the eye, and getting paid for it. Insubordination had ranked pretty high on my list at the DA's office. Now I could write my own ticket, call my own shots. I was ready for it. I had a hat, a gun, and a coat. Maybe what I needed was some life insurance, but what I wanted was a cigarette. I'd have to wait until Gower's drugstore reopened.

"I charge twenty-five dollars a day and expenses," I said. "Plus eight cents a mile for my car."

"I'd pay anything to get George out," she said.

"And I'll need one hundred dollars as a retainer."

"Of course." She reached over for a candy jar. It was shaped like a snowman. She lifted off his ceramic top hat and took out a fold of bills. She had plenty of Fort Knox salad in the house from last night.

I slipped the money into my wallet. It was like feeding a hungry stomach. I settled back into the chair.

"Let's figure Potter was killed by someone who hated him, or by someone who wanted his money," I said. "Or maybe by someone who hated your husband and wanted to frame him. I know Potter wouldn't win any Chamber of Commerce awards, but did he have any particular enemies?"

"No one liked him, not really." She paused and twisted her wedding ring about her finger. "But I don't know that anyone hated him in particular."

"Eight thousand dollars was reported missing from the Building and Loan. What if Potter had got hold of the money, and someone found out Potter had it?"

Mary Bailey puckered her brow as though this was the first time she'd thought of it. It was hard to tell how much she knew, or if she were just following my reasoning.

"How about George?" I said. "Would anybody want to frame him?"

"You saw how the town turned out for him."

"But somebody had socked him pretty good in the mouth. Who?"

"Mr. Walsh. Husband of one of the teachers. George shouted at her for letting Zuzu, that's my little girl, go home with her coat unbuttoned. That's how she caught a cold. The Walshes live over on Oakdale Street. The yellow house with white shutters at the end of the road."

I doubted a little girl's case of the sniffles and a grown man's bloody nose added up to murder. But in this place, who could tell. It was a crazy kind of town, where you could call a kid "Zuzu" and no one even batted an eyelash. To hell with these hicks, I thought. They made me sick. But they were writing my paycheck. I stood up. So did Mrs. Bailey.

Mrs. Bailey twisted the window cord around her finger. She looked better than any wife whose husband had just been carted off for murder had any right to look.

"You'd make a good cop," I said.

"I make a better wife." She paused and let go of the cord. "I wouldn't see George just yet, Mr. Incles. He isn't himself. The strain."

I said goodbye, put on my hat, and headed into the slushy street. I got behind the wheel and drove a few blocks across town. I sat in my car and thought. I drank my dinner, alone. Christmas Day hung gray and cold over Bedford Falls like a hangover everyone shared. I figured we all needed to sleep it off. But I had work to do.

And it looked like I wasn't the only one.

CHAPTER EIGHT

A single light was burning in the window of Gower's drug store. Gower was one Santa Claus who did his appointed rounds last night. It didn't make sense for him to be in the shop on Christmas Day, so I figured I'd pay him a visit. I wondered exactly what business he'd had last night with Henry Potter.

The drugstore was shingled pale gray, with a broad windowed shop front. A red and white striped awning was still up, and its fringe hung frozen in the winter cold. I went up to the door and knocked. The bell on the other side of the door chimed. I watched my breath. The minutes went by so slowly I wondered if the hands of a watch can get frost-bite too. I was half-dazed by my own fanciful wit when the door opened.

"Wh-whaddaya want?" Mr. Gower said. He was looking right at me, but he took a long second to focus. He was chewing on an unlit cigar, and a five o'clock shadow had settled in several hours early. His breath was about 60 proof.

"Mr. Gower, it's me, Richard Incles. I was driving by and noticed the light on. And I wondered if -"

"You wondered! You got no business here, fella." He stepped backwards from the doorway. "What are you selling anyway?"

"I'm not selling, Mr. Gower. I'm buying." I took out my wallet to demonstrate my good will, and followed him into the drugstore. He was muttering to himself and didn't seem to notice.

At first glance, the drugstore was clean and orderly. The far wall was lined with shelves, each stocked with foot-high containers. A few of them were marked with a skull and crossbones. The highest shelf had had a pretty good going over, though, and it was easy to guess what had been on it. The counter below was littered with a few half-empty liquor bottles.

"Mr. Gower, I'm working on behalf of Mrs. Bailey and her husband."

Gower sunk himself into the stool at the end of the counter. He put his face in his hands. "They got George," he said. He started to sob. Then he put his hands flat on the counter. "George in prison, where I would be if he hadn't..." He looked me in the eyes. "George saved my life, and someone else's too. Long time ago, but I won't ever forget it."

I sat on the stool beside him, and pulled a bottle out of my coat. "Maybe you'd like to talk about it."

"Talk about it - that was one thing George swore he'd never do. He was true to his word." Gower took a swig from the bottle. "The day it happened was the day I got the news. A telegram that my boy was dead. The influenza got him, his first term at university. How would you feel, mister, if it was you? I took a drink in the back room. I thought it would steady my nerves, and then I didn't care what it did. I had to go about my business that day. Mrs. Blaine was waiting for a box of capsules. They had the diphtheria there, you see. I mixed a batch of capsules, but from the wrong bottle. From poison. I would have killed that Blaine boy, if George hadn't caught it." Gower shook his head. "George never told a living soul. And he was only a kid then too."

He looked at me, to share in his amazement. Let's say I

was interested. Gower took another swig. "George arrested."

"Mr. Gower, you delivered some medicine to Potter last night. Could I have a sample?"

"What for?" He got up from the stool and went in back of the counter. "You got a pain in your legs that acts up when the cold sets in? Or you think maybe I made the same mistake twice? Potter's medicine I didn't mix. It comes prepared." Gower shot a small blue and white box over to me. "He insisted they did wonders for his aches, but there's nothing to them but flour and sugar." He sat down again.

I opened a capsule up, dipped my finger in it, and tasted. Gower was right, at least about the box he had given me. I slipped it into my pocket. "Who do you think killed Potter?"

"Nobody," Gower said. "Nobody but his own greed. He choked trying to eat his own money." He laughed. He rolled his eyes toward the ceiling and kept laughing until it became a tired rasp and he had to stop. He put his hands on the counter and hunched his shoulders up. His eyes were still bleary.

"You know that for a fact?" I said.

He nodded.

"How?"

"It must have been Ernie," Gower said. "That's it. Ernie Bishop told me."

"You sure about that?"

"The whole town knows by now, son. We're a small place, and things have a way of getting around."

"Like diphtheria and poisoned capsules."

Gower looked at me.

It was possible Gower had killed Potter to help George, and the killing backfired, or killed Potter as revenge for what Potter had recently done to Bailey. Either way, Gower was worth keeping in mind.

"Have another swig of cheer," I suggested.

"No, thanks," Gower said. His chin was steady. His eyes were clearing up. It's a terrible thing to watch a man grow sober before your eyes.

"Well, then, you just keep it," I said, patting the bottle. "I'll buy a pack of Camels, if you don't mind."

"Okay." He shuffled over to the counter and tossed a pack onto the counter. "That'll be thirty-five cents, with tax. Includes those pills you took."

I fished out the coins and headed out the door into Christmas Day in Bedford Falls. I needed some solid food for once. The light was on at Martini's. I had a steak, and tried to ignore the carolers in the back. I took my time eating and then went up to the bar to order a scotch. Martini was behind the counter.

"George didn't do it," a woman in front of me said.

"And so what if he did," her companion responded. "Potter's no great loss."

A wizened-face man nodded. "Yeah, I'm with George whether he did it, or he didn't."

"If he did, he shouldn't get jail," another man said. "He should get a medal."

Gower scuttled in, and went up to the bar. He had a fresh shave, and now he looked purified by age and suffering. He saw me but gave no sign of recognition. He leaned over the bar and had a word with Martini, who nodded, accepted a few bills from Gower, and then looked up.

"George Bailey is no killer," Martini said. "Everybody, listen, before we close today. Mr. Gower is buying a round, in honor of our friend George Bailey."

The grouchy beefcake of a bartender hoisted a bottle and started pouring. When he got to me, he jerked the bottle up too quickly and a few drops of liquor spilled onto my hand.

"You've just had one on me," I said. I grinned.

He straightened up to about six foot three. That made him one inch taller than I was. "You know, someday that's what I'm going to miss about this joint. Wise guys like you who think they're a regular vaudeville act."

Gower raised his glass. "To George Bailey, a great friend and the salt of the earth."

I raised a glass myself. It was a comedown from being toasted by a war hero brother as the richest man in town, I guess, but it was still something.

CHAPTER NINE

I woke up the next morning to rain. It drummed so hard on the roof it made me think of a thousand skeletons dancing a jitterbug. I stood up and looked out the window. I had the taste of rye in my mouth and $97 and change in my pocket. I was ready for anything.

I shaved and dressed and drove over to Ernie's garage. It was a few blocks across town, on Jefferson. By the time I got there, it looked like Ernie had already put in a few hours. He was wiping his hands on a rag and whistling to a tune on the radio when I pulled up and got out of the car.

"Help you, mister?" he said.

"I hope so. This old wreck of mine has been giving me some trouble. Mind taking a look?"

"Sure thing." Ernie opened the hood. I glanced around the place. The garage was cramped and ramshackle, with loose parts and tools scattered over a ledge. There was an old-fashioned stove in the near corner. Hanging on a nail on the wall above it was a calendar which featured the schedule for a race track. Beside the calendar there was a pay phone, and below that, by my feet, a dented-up metal tray with a penciled sign stuck on it, "Lost and Found." I spotted a black derby, a toaster, a half-empty flask of perfume and a few mismatched earrings.

Ernie poked his head out from under the hood. "Crazy the stuff people leave behind in a cab. I swear, if I saved everything I found back there I'd have enough geegaws to outfit Macy's." He shook his head. "So far I can't find a darned thing wrong. But I'll keep looking, mister - "

"Incles," I said.

"I'm Ernie Bishop. You new in town?"

"You could say that. I'm a friend of George Bailey's."

"I know most of George's friends. Oh, I get it - you're that private eye." I could tell he was impressed. "You used to work for the DA's, until..." He lapsed into silence.

"I'm flattered. How'd you know so much about me?"

"We're a small town mister and things -"

"Have a way of getting around. So I hear."

"It's a quiet place, and any news is big news."

"A murder like Potter's would be pretty big news in any town. Shot three times. Once through the head, once through the heart, and once through the wallet." I took out a cigarette and looked for a match. "It was the wallet that did it."

Ernie laughed like an asthmatic. "That's pretty funny, mister," he said when he was able to breathe again. "I knew it was a joke all along."

"Really?" I lit the cigarette and looked at him through a haze of smoke. "How?"

"Potter choked on his own money. Everybody knows that."

"What else does everybody know, Ernie?"

"Huh?"

"And how does everybody know it? There's only one way for someone outside the law to know how Potter died."

"Oh, not if they know Bert the cop," Ernie said. "If he knows something, and if he knows you, he gets to talking. When there's a cup of coffee and a slice of pie in front of him, you may as well be reading the official police file direct. But it doesn't do anybody any harm."

I hoped it would do me some good. I pressed on. "You think George did it?"

Ernie straightened his back, put his hands in his pockets and looked at the floor. "No." He raised his eyes to mine. "And some people think it was good riddance."

"Including you?"

"Not enough to do anything about it." He was looking a little less friendly and a lot less stupid. It was hard to tell if the dark lines on his face were grease marks or a frown. The phone rang. "Excuse me," he said.

I went over to my car but I kept an ear open.

"Hi," he said. Then he lowered his voice, but he was clearly new to that game. He tried to keep his voice hushed and toneless but it kept drifting in and out of decibel ranges like a radio searching for a signal. "Uh-huh, sure...I can get you the money no problem. Good thing the wife's out of town...she doesn't know a thing. Okay then. Midnight, doll. Talk to you later." He hung up and was like a new man. He started to whistle, and gave a dance step before he remembered I was there.

"Just a bit of business," he said.

I got the picture. Boy meets girl, boy loses girl, boy gets girl, boy meets second girl who makes him forget about the first one, and depletes family bank balance in the process. How his wife felt about it was no skin off my nose. But Ernie had something to hide. I wondered what her name was. And I wondered what else he knew about Potter.

Ernie went over to my car and poked around the engine briefly. "Mister, the only thing I see is a loose fan belt. Tighten that up in a jiff, and off you go."

I kept looking at him through the smoke of my cigarette. Under the unshaded bulb, Ernie's hat cast a grotesque shadow onto the garage floor. The nicest people in Bedford Falls were casting shadows as dark as the shadows the nicest people cast anyplace else.

CHAPTER TEN

I headed over to the TipTop cafe for a late breakfast. The TipTop overlooked the county jail and I could tell when the cop on guard was out rounding up renegade doughnuts. I figured I could get past whoever else was on watch by flashing my old ID from the DA's. When I got George's story, I would go from there.

I settled in to the front booth at the TipTop and ordered two fried eggs, home-style potatoes, a side plate of bacon and a bottomless cup of coffee.

"New in town?" the waitress said as she poured me my third go of black coffee. "Don't think I've seen you before."

"Just got here Christmas Eve," I said. She had copper brown hair drawn back like a ballet dancer's. But her shoulders were more like a lumberjack's. She looked strong and cheery, as though she could clear out a pine forest along the north-forty, and be back for a griddleful of flapjacks and syrup before eight. She wore bright red lipstick that clashed with her hair, and her fingernails were painted magenta. She smiled and turned back to the counter. The cup of coffee may have been bottomless but she wasn't.

I kept my eye on the street. A blue van pulled up in front of a butcher shop, and a stout red-faced man in a striped apron came out and ran a few boxes from the van into the shop. The traffic lights changed. The rain bounced off the street into the gutters. Women hurried by, their bags heavy with shopping and their heads tucked deep into the collars of their coats. Then at the entrance of the jail, Bert the cop appeared. He was about to leave the building. He had a goofy grin on his face, and he was talking to somebody still inside. He looked at the rain and shook his head.

I dropped a bill on the counter, and pulled on my coat. I had seen what I came here for.

So had someone else.

"Been meaning to talk to you, stranger," a voice purred into my ear. It was a voice like silk, spun smooth, but I bet it could be pretty raw when it wanted.

I turned to face her. I was looking straight into the hat top of Violet Bick. Amazing the hats women will wear. This one perched her head, slightly askew, like a panicked ferret ready to jump ship. But the rest of her was worth looking at, her legs especially. She was trouble.

"I have something I need to tell you. About George," she said. "Got a minute?"

"It'll have to wait, sister," I said. Across the street, Bert was heading down the sidewalk, in the direction of Anderson's department store.

"Huh?" Her brows drew together and her nostrils flared.

"Meet me at Martini's. Tonight." I kept my eyes on Bert and I didn't wait for her answer as I headed out the door.

CHAPTER ELEVEN

The Bedford Falls police station was a small brick building a few hundred yards from the main road. I pushed on the green door, and it swung open heavily. The hinges gave a slow pneumatic hiss, releasing a pocket of air that had been trapped there since Teddy Roosevelt went riding up Pork Chop Hill. At the front desk, a fresh-faced kid sat reading a comic book. His wrists stuck out several inches from his shirtsleeves, and were about the width of a pencil.

"Help you, mister," he said. He didn't put the comic book aside.

"I need to speak to Mr. George Bailey." I got out my wallet and opened it up to my DA badge. I pushed it across the table to him.

He gave the badge a glance, and got up, his feet nearly tripping over the chair legs. He led me into a small back room. The far corner was taken up with a jail cell. There was a flat bed a few feet off the floor. George Bailey sat at the edge of it.

"Mary? Ma-" he called out. Then he saw we weren't Mary. His eyes had deep shadows underneath them. He would need more than a night's sleep to get rid of them, maybe a lifetime's. He didn't belong in this kind of trouble. He wasn't built for it.

"Mr. Bailey," the kid said. "Anything I can get you?"

Bailey shook his head. The kid went away.

"Mr. Bailey, I'm -" I began.

"I know who you are. My wife told me to expect you." He was stuttering slightly. He raked his hair back with his hand. It was a long thin hand. His eyes were all pupils, glittering and black. "I thought my troubles with Potter were all over. Now I'm in a worse fix than ever."

"So's he, I guess."

"Yeah, I guess," Bailey said. He laughed, briefly. Then he stared at me. He stood up and gripped the bars of the cell. He was over six feet, as lean as a stalk of celery and about as imposing.

"Let's start at the beginning," I said. "I know eight thousand dollars was missing. That's why Potter had me brought down here in the first place. Do you know who took it?"

"I - I lost it. It must have fallen onto the street somehow. Or got thrown out by accident. I don't know."

"You have no idea who might have picked it up?"

"No sir."

"When you found it was missing what did you do?"

"I went looking all over town for it. So did Uncle Billy. He's treasurer of the Building and Loan. We re-traced hi-my steps that day. We couldn't find a nickel of it. I went home, but I couldn't bring myself to tell my wife. So I went out again, and I tried to borrow the money from Mr. Potter."

"You saw him in his office that night?"

"Yes. He went and called the DA's office right in front of me. I ran out. Went to Martini's for a drink."

"How'd you get the bloody lip?"

"Oh, that. Earlier that night, when I was home, I shouted over the phone at one of the kids' teachers. Mrs. Walsh. It turned out the lug sitting next to me at Martini's was Mr. Walsh. He heard my name and he hadn't liked the way I'd spoken to his wife, so he let me have it. Can't say I blame him. And then I wandered off, to the bridge." He stopped talking, and blinked.

"Go on," I said.

"Don't tell anybody this."

"Okay."

"I was at the end of my rope. Potter told me I was worth more dead than alive. And he was right. I kept looking down in the water - it had me in some kind of spell or trance, it felt like. I was about to jump, when another body hurtled straight past me, into the water. I had to dive in to fish him out."

"Who's him?"

"Clarence Odbody. I never met him before, but he knew all about me. Boy, did he. We got to talking in the toll keeper's shack. Clarence convinced me I really have a wonderful life. Showed it to me - like in the pictures! And when he was done, I ran home clear across town. I even wished Potter a Merry Christmas. Knocked on his window." Bailey smiled grimly.

"Odbody," I said. "So he was with you the night Potter got killed. When you were scampering home, where did he run off to?"

"I can't say."

"Where can I get hold of him?"

"You can't."

"Why not?"

"He's gone home."

"Where's that?"

"Far away from here."

"It can't be that far."

"It's farther than you think," George said. "He flew there."

"Through a blizzard, like an angel, I suppose." It was pretty clear this Odbody didn't exist. Bailey couldn't deliver him, and it was too screwball a name to be for real.

40

But on the other hand who would make up a name that goofy?

"Hey, how'd you know he was an angel?" George said. "Mister, you're some detective."

"Anybody else at the bridge?"

"The toll keeper, Just don't tell anybody about...you know." He pointed heavenward.

"Then people came by your house and donated money. Did you leave your house after that?"

"Yes, sir."

"Where did you go?"

"I went outside to look at the sky. The stars, the moon, everything! I know I have a few friends up there too." He smiled. He gripped the bars and drew his face a few inches closer to mine. His eyes became serious and his voice lowered as though he were telling a secret. "You ever see snow fall in the moonlight, Mr. Incles?"

"Skip it, bud." I was convinced he was off his nut at least one-third of the time. But I liked him. Even if he was guilty, which it looked like he was.

I stood up. The door swung open. Callaghan barreled through, with one of his deputies in tow. When he saw I was there, his face was as friendly as a loaded .38.

"What do you think you're doing here?" Callaghan said.

"Mr. Incles is a friend of the family," Bailey said.

"You've got a lot of friends," Callaghan said.

"I like to think so," George said.

"Don't think so much. Just answer the questions. I mean my questions. Not his." Callaghan turned to me. "Beat it, pal. You've got no business here."

"I could make it my business."

"And I could issue a warrant for your arrest. Interfering with a police investigation."

"You wouldn't want to. Then you'd have to question me and your questions would then become my questions. Get it?"

Callaghan's eyes went blank. His hands floundered a bit

at the end of his sleeves like trout on the end of a hook. His deputy had a notepad in the palm of his hand and was scribbling away.

"Ray," Callaghan said sharply. "What's all that chicken-scratching? I haven't asked Bailey anything yet."

"Yes sir," the deputy said.

I was on my way out.

CHAPTER TWELVE

The sky was as low and gray as the ceiling in a flophouse basement. I went back to my car and had a shot of lunch. I slipped the bottle back into my coat pocket. It was just past three o'clock. The sky was already getting dark. Night would soon fall, as well as more rain. The drifts of snow were turning into gray slush.

I drove over to the north side of town. Bedford Bridge was about sixty yards long. It had a narrow iron railing on each side. The toll keeper's shack was attached to the near end of the bridge. The shack was small and dark. There was a single yellow light in the front window. I parked in back, by the trunk of an oak tree that had been split in two. I pulled my coat collar up and ran to the door and knocked.

A wiry, middle-aged man answered. Over his black denims, he was wearing a pea coat, a coarsely knitted scarf, and a train conductor's cap. I gathered that was his in-door attire, because he had a mug of what smelled like fresh-burnt coffee still in his hand.

His face had no expression, but it wasn't mean. It was more as if he had lived alone so long there was no point in having facial expressions anymore. He waited for me to speak. He may not say much, I figured, but what he does say I'd be willing to buy.

"My name's Incles. I'm a friend of George Bailey's."

The toll keeper kept his eyes on me. Without stirring himself an inch, he shot a stream of tobacco a half-foot from my right shoe. Then he stepped aside from the door. I took that to mean I was okay to go in. The room was sparsely furnished. In the middle of the floor, there was a black wood-burning stove. On a front burner, a pot of coffee sputtered. A couple of mismatched chairs and a cabinet were jammed against the walls. A bare light bulb hung from the ceiling.

He got out a mug from the cabinet and held it out to me. He jerked his chin in the direction of the pot-bellied stove.

"Help yourself," he said. I poured myself a muddy coffee. He pulled a chair towards the stove and sat down. I did the same.

"You know George Bailey?" I said.

"Heard of him."

"He's in some trouble."

"Heard that too."

"I'm working for him. I'm trying to get him out of his mess, and I thought you might be able to help. Did anything happen here Christmas Eve?"

"Christmas Eve?" he said.

"Day before yesterday."

He thought about it. "That there pipe burst and I had a time fixing it."

"What time was George Bailey here?"

"Nope."

"You're not sure when it was," I said.

"Nope. I mean yep. He wasn't here that night any time. Or any other night."

I took a sip of coffee. That was a mistake but I had a remedy. I pulled the pint of rye from my coat pocket. "How about a drink?"

He held his mug out to me.

"What about his friend?" I said. "Name of Odbody. You remember him?"

"Nope." He took a long swig. "Never heard of him. I don't get many visitors around here, and I'd remember it. I don't know who's been telling you George Bailey was out this way that night, but they're lying." He put down his mug and shot a stream of tobacco juice into the stove. "And if he wants, I'm willing to testify to that."

I had another drink with him, and then I drove back to the boarding house. I parked across the street and lit a cigarette. I had plenty to think about. I had a client who lied to me, or was so far gone he didn't know he was lying. Mrs. Bailey had to be told if she didn't already know. Maybe he was covering something up. Maybe he'd been with Violet Bick that night.

I had my key this time, and let myself into my room. Somebody else had gotten there first.

CHAPTER THIRTEEN

Violet Bick was sitting at the edge of the bed.

"Hello, Goldilocks," I said. I hung my coat on the door hook, and turned to face her again. "Who's been sleeping in my bed?"

She smiled, the slow and easy smile of a woman who is used to being liked. "Mrs. Parker let me in. I told her you were expecting me." She held out a business card from her coral-dipped fingernails. "So you know where to find me." The card was thin white linen, and lettered in curvy black script. It read: "Violet's Beautee Shoppe, Bedford Falls. For ladies and gents." The card was pretty fancy for this town. So was she. She drew back her hand. The heavy scent of floral cologne surrounded her slightest motion like a trained military phalanx.

"Mrs. Parker ask you anything else?" I said. "Her bloodhounds prowl the hallways day and night, and they're pretty fierce. You have to throw them a bit of information wrapped up in butcher's paper to get them off your trail."

"I got by them alright," she said. "This time. Mrs. Parker did tell me one thing though." She pouted. "No visitors after seven o'clock." She lowered her chin and smiled up at me through her lashes. She had contralto eyes. They spoke in the lower register. Her legs covered both registers. They stretched out in front of her like a summer afternoon. She crossed them. That didn't make them any shorter.

"As soon as I found out what happened, I had to talk to you." She shifted her legs to the opposite side, the side I couldn't see.

"Uh-huh."

"What do you mean, 'uh-huh'?"

"What do you mean, 'what happened'?"

"Mr. Potter dead."

"Or George Bailey being arrested?"

"What's the difference?" I could tell she was already liking me a lot less. She paused a moment. With the flat of her palms, she smoothed the wrinkles in her lap. She began again.

"Everybody's saying Potter was killed by money," she said. "That somebody pushed money down his throat, and it was a lot of money."

"Uh-huh."

"Uh-huh that's what they say or uh-huh that's how it happened?"

"Uh-huh."

She frowned. "There was something about a ledger book, too, they said. That Potter was making an entry in his book when he was killed."

"Who's they?"

"Why, everybody in town," she said. "A lot of people seem to think George did it." She paused again.

"Uh-huh."

"Do you think so?"

"Do you?" I said.

"Look mister, you've got an awfully funny way of acting. I don't like your manners." She stood up. Her hat bristled at me.

"Now that you mention it, I'm not wild about yours. I didn't ask to see you. You wanted to see me. Don't get me wrong. I don't mind seeing you. Not at all. It's a cold winter day and maybe we could have got a little cozy. But don't waste your time trying to interrogate me."

She smoothed her forehead with her hand.

"What's your angle?" I said. "Were you with George Bailey that night?"

She lowered her chin and looked up at me steadily. This time it was no pose. "I could be. If that's what it takes to get George off."

"You've just offered yourself up on a platter," I said. "You do that for every guy?"

"Why, I ought to -" She chipped at the air with her right hand.

"I'd offer to leave at this point but it is my room."

She steadied her hat. She looked around, as if searching for some stray shred of dignity that might have fallen to the floor like a silken scarf. But the carpet was bare. She opened the door.

"I'll have to get back to the shop," she said.

Then she turned to face me. Her jaw went firmer and her eyes focused on mine squarely. They were the eyes you see taking aim above a pistol. "I know George Bailey didn't kill Potter." She gave each word a hard, equal emphasis. She shut the door behind her.

She had nice legs, I had to admit. There were a few questions I wouldn't mind asking her, like how she knew what she said she knew, and what exactly she was trying to find out. And why she was so willing to give George Bailey an alibi. I'd have to watch her. There were worse jobs I could think of.

CHAPTER FOURTEEN

The next morning dawned bright and freezing. The weak sun shone down on Bedford Falls with an ingratiating warmth, like the smile of a short-term buddy who has hopes of hitting you up for a loan. I washed, shaved, and got dressed. I headed over to the TipTop cafe, where the lumberjack waitress with the magenta nails brought me my fried eggs and toast. I got back in my car and drove over to 320 Sycamore. I didn't look forward to what I would have to do.

Mrs. Bailey answered the door. Her hands were floury, and she wiped them on her apron. She smiled as if she hadn't a care in the world, as if now that I was on the case and sure to get her husband off, she could bake pies and a batch of sugar cookies for the kids.

"Come in, please, Mr. Incles," she said. She led me into the living room. "I was hoping you'd stop by, to give us any news. Please." She indicated a chair and I sat down.

"Mrs. Bailey, I'm going to have to tell you a few things, and tell them to you straight."

She sunk into the chair opposite me and lifted her jaw. She nodded. I was right the first time I saw her. When the chips were down, she was no Little Red Riding Hood.

49

"It's George. His alibi doesn't check out for the night Potter was killed. He told me he was in the toll keeper's shack that night with a fellow named Odbody. Trouble is the toll keeper doesn't know a thing about it."

"He's told you about Clarence." Her mouth went tense and her hands clenched into tight little fists.

"He's told me a story about how he jumped into the river to save this fellow, Clarence Odbody, and that Odbody then proceeded to convince George his life was worth living. He's made it clear that I won't be able to reach Odbody. The toll keeper is ready to testify that George wasn't there that night, or Odbody, either, if that testimony will help clear your husband. Except you and I know it won't."

I paused. If I had a drink, I would have taken a good swig at this point. "I don't like being lied to, Mrs. Bailey. I don't know if your husband even knows he's lying anymore. But I can't work for a client who's stringing me along."

Mrs. Bailey brushed her forehead with her right hand. "George hasn't been, well, quite the same since that night. He's almost unhinged. It's the strain he's been under. He's told me the same story, Mr. Incles, so I'm sure he doesn't mean to mislead you. Let me get something."

She went over to a low-shelved bookcase wedged in behind the door, and came back with a white leather-bound volume. She held it out to me. "He showed this to me on Christmas Eve. Look at the fly-leaf."

It was a copy of *The Adventures of Tom Sawyer*. It looked like an antique. Across the fly-leaf was penned an inscription: "Dear George, Remember no man is a failure who has friends. Thanks for the wings. Love Clarence." The handwriting was oversized and rounded. It was the handwriting of a child, or an idiot.

Mrs. Bailey closed the book. "George must have written that out himself, when he was in some kind of trance. But he does believe what he's been saying."

Mrs. Bailey was a nice woman, whomever she had married. I wondered why George would make such a point of showing this book to his wife. Unless he needed to cover up some get-together he'd had with Violet Bick that night, and he hoped the book would be proof he had been with "Clarence Odbody." Or possibly Gower's drug arsenal had finally driven him around the bend, permanently. Or maybe he was getting things in place for an insanity defense. It was hard to figure but I knew this much: there was more to George than met the eye.

"He's in trouble," Mrs. Bailey said. "But he's no killer. That's why you've got to help him."

I had helped him more than I was comfortable with. I was still thinking things over as we stood up and walked into the front room.

"Can you think of anyone he'd know named Clarence?" I said. "Or something similar?"

"Not a soul."

"It's not the most common name, but not unheard of either. George picked it up from somewhere."

The front door opened. Mrs. Bailey's mother appeared at the threshold. Bailey's kid brother was at her side. He held the door open and followed her in. I took a close look at him. He had a lean face, with a dark straight brow and a narrow nose. He was small but powerfully built, and he moved with an athlete's confidence. He had a suit from the cleaners slung over his left shoulder. He hung the suit up in the hall closet, and took off his coat. He was wearing a college sweater. Mrs. Bailey's mother nodded at us each in turn without smiling.

"I thought I'd start dinner," she said.

"Harry, this is Mr. Incles. He's the man I told you about," Mrs. Bailey said. "Mr. Incles, this is Harry, George's little brother. And I think you've already met my mother."

Harry gripped my hand. He smiled. He had a lot of teeth. "The old private eye himself. No magnifying glass or

51

deer stalker cap? What have you found out that'll get my big brother out of this mess?"

"I'll go over that with you later," Mrs. Bailey said.

"I think it's time we went over it now," he said. He looked at me. He was used to doing the talking and used to being listened to. His eyes were still bright blue, but the jocularity had dropped out of them. "I'll tell you the truth, Mr. -" He waved a hand in a gesture of forgetfulness.

"Incles. Same as it was a minute ago."

"It's been two days now and George is in as much trouble as ever. I just don't know if you're the right man for the job."

"It doesn't matter what you know and don't know. Though I am surprised you admit there's anything you don't know. Let's get one thing straight. You didn't hire me. Mrs. Bailey did, on her husband's behalf. And at this point, I would say George is lucky to have any detective pounding the sidewalks for him."

"A tough-talking gumshoe. You really make me laugh." His face betrayed no mirth. "Maybe if you had ever seen any real action like me, or Marty or somebody, you'd have reason to talk."

Mrs. Hatch put her hands to her eyes. A sob escaped from her. Harry winced, but he stood his ground. Mrs. Bailey put an arm around her, but the older woman ran from the room.

Mrs. Bailey gave Harry an angry look. "You know how that kind of talk upsets mother." She turned and faced me. "Marty was my brother, Mr. Incles. He helped capture Remagen Bridge. He always had a weak heart, and, well, he never made it back. My mother hasn't been the same since." She looked again at Harry, less angry this time. "You just don't understand all that's happened. We need Mr. Incles more than ever." She straightened her skirt. "I'll see to mother." She left the room.

"Good work, soldier," I said.

"Mr. Incles, it's clear you've done all you can -"

"No. I haven't. And when you bother to listen to your sister-in-law, you'll find that out, and you'll be glad I'm on your brother's side. Maybe you better consider how you look in all of this, soldier boy."

"Say what you mean, mister."

"The night you come roaring into town, first time in years, and through a blizzard, to come to the aid of your beloved brother, is the night Potter gets it. Maybe there's no limit to the loyalty the Bailey boys feel to each other. Maybe you killed George's worst enemy for him. And maybe you'll need to hire me yourself, in a few days time, when the boys in blue get to thinking like that."

"Are you trying to tell me -"

"Oh I know you're a hero. With a medal and everything. But a battle zone isn't the same as the scene of a crime. There are a few areas of Bedford Falls I'd advise you not to invade."

"Cute. Who writes your script?"

"So long, soldier," I said. "See you around. I'll show myself out."

We stared at each other a moment. He clenched his jaw a notch tighter. Then he turned away.

CHAPTER FIFTEEN

The sun was shining a little less brightly than it had been, but it was still the kind of day with enough snap and sparkle in it to make you feel that a brisk walk would clear your head. That is, if your head wasn't too full of things to think about in the first place. Mine was. I headed over to Martini's.

Martini's looked different today, plainer. It was as if a strawberry blonde with the kind of a curves a man can get lost in had woken up the next day with her curves well-hidden, and her hair pulled back as primly as a librarian's. The bar was closed.

"Not open for another hour, mister," Martini said. "But food's ready. Linguine special. You sit here maybe?" He pointed to a small table in the corner, and smiled.

I sat down and looked around. The place was filling up. A few of these people had been at George Bailey's house Christmas Eve. One of them must know something, I figured. Martini brought me a plate of linguine. I ate my way through it and bided my time.

The door opened, and on a blast of cold and a ray of sunshine, Uncle Billy came in. He trundled straight over to the bar stool that was nearest my table.

"Bar's not open yet, Mr. Billy," Martini said.

"Oh no bother. I'll just wait," Billy said. He smiled nervously. His bushy white eyebrows appeared to surprise even themselves. He fidgeted. He was still wearing an out-of-season white suit and a straw hat. His pockets were crammed full of papers. An envelope fell to the floor. He didn't notice.

I went over to him. I picked up the envelope from the floor. It was addressed to the Bailey Bros. Building and Loan, and had no return address. "You dropped this," I said.

He looked at me. His glasses slipped down his nose a fraction. His eyes were clear blue circles of fear. With the flat of his hand, he pushed his glasses back up. "Thanks, mister." He peered at me closer. "Do I know you?"

"I'm a friend of George Bailey's. Maybe you can help him out."

"I'd do anything for George," Billy said. His fear had melted. "I'm his uncle, Billy."

"Anything?" I said. I let the suggestion hang a minute in the air.

"You name it. If Potter were alive right now, I'd go spit in his eye myself. When I think about George, I - why, I hated Potter at least as much as George did. We sure showed him though."

"How's that?" I said.

"How? By building houses. By earning medals."

"Not by killing him."

Billy raised his eyebrows. His eyes became a frozen blue again and he clammed up. I decided I better change tack.

"What happened to that eight thousand dollars?" I said.

"I don't know. Nobody knows. I - George- it got lost that's all. What did George tell you? Whatever it was, that's the truth." He turned away from me and faced straight ahead.

I looked at him. He was a cagey fellow. A small time

operator who had gotten pretty good at playing the village idiot. Maybe he was tired of playing it. It was hard to tell just what he knew, but easy to see he knew a lot.

"Five dollars," I said.

"Five do- I don't carry that sort of money around with me. Not anymore. No sir. I've learned my lesson, thank you."

"Five dollars," I said as though I hadn't heard him. I pulled out my wallet. I arranged five one dollar bills in front of me.

"Mister, you better be careful with that stuff," Billy said. He looked behind him. "What are you putting money out like that for?"

"I like playing solitaire. Unless you'd like to join in."

"Then it wouldn't be solitaire," he said.

"So I'll play a different game. Let's say I ask a question and every time you give the answer, you take a dollar bill."

He smiled as though now he understood. Then his face froze up. "I can't do that."

He was pretty good at this, I had to admit. "Make it two dollars."

"No," he said. "Hey, that's an answer." He helped himself to two bills. He smiled at me like a triumphant child. "I liked that game just fine. You know another one?"

"Yes. It's called let's skip the monkeyshine and get down to business."

Billy drew his shoulders back and frowned. "I don't like the sound of that."

Mr. Martini entered behind the bar from the backroom. He polished a few glasses, and announced, "Open for business. Now what can I get you?"

"Oh, I like the sound of that." Billy rolled his eyes at me.

"Okay, Mr. Martini," I said. "Two doubles. This time it's on me." I pushed some money in front of him.

Martini smiled and served us each a drink.

"Where's the barman?" I said. "I mean the graduate of

the Sing-Sing School of Charm and Etiquette."

"Nick? He's not here no more," Martini said. "Got new work, some kind handyman for the bank." He straightened his sleeves. "Better for him, maybe, to get away from the bar some. I wish him luck."

"He brightens a place up like nobody's business," I said.

Martini grinned despite himself.

"Mr. Martini, you wouldn't know anything about Henry Potter would you?"

"Why you ask?"

"I'm working on behalf of George Bailey."

Martini put down the glass in his hand and raised his right hand. He pointed his index finger into the air, like a teacher giving a lesson. "Mr. Potter was a mean man. Greedy. I'm glad you asked me. If he had his way, I'd still be renting a shack from him that wasn't fit for a pig sty. George stood up to him, for all of us."

"So you're not too broken up about Potter."

"In a way, I am," Martini said. "Look where he got George now."

"Where did Potter live?"

"That big house by the river. With an iron fence posted all over with signs, No Trespassing. Beware of the Dog. Why he do that, I don't know. No one wanted to go where he was."

A few customers had come in and sat down the other end of the bar. Martini went over to serve them.

"You asking about Potter?" a jowly man at the next table said.

The man had his wallet in his hand and was counting out money for his bill. I had seen him at Bailey's house on Christmas Eve. He wore a soft plaid scarf folded inside the neck of his coat. It was the only soft and colored thing about him. The rest of him was gray and solidly fat, as though he could sit in a tub full of ice cubes and never feel a thing.

"Nobody knew Potter," he said. "Didn't have a friend or a relative. Didn't make a bit of difference to anyone, at least not of a kind they would want to remember." He straightened his hat. "I'd be surprised if anybody could tell you a thing about him except his bank balance. It ought to be his epitaph." He looked at me as he fastened the top button of his coat. "Well, so long," he said. I watched him leave.

"Who was that?" I said.

"Tom Partridge," Billy said. "Principal of the high school."

Then he took another swig. "Potter not make a difference to anyone," he sputtered, half to himself. "I'll tell you one difference Potter made. The reason George stayed with the Building and Loan was so there'd be somebody to stand up to Potter. George had big plans, once upon a time. He was going to see South America, the Yukon, Peking. And then build cities and skyscrapers and all manner of things. Well, Potter changed all that. Potter trapped George here the same as though he had chained him to Main Street hand and foot." Billy finished his drink with a loud emphatic slurp.

Callaghan didn't have to worry. George's friends just had to open their mouths and George would be on his way to the chair. I was worried. And not just because clients have a strange reluctance to pay for their own murder conviction.

CHAPTER SIXTEEN

It was about two thirty when I headed out in the fading winter sunlight. I went into Gower's and bought myself another pack of Camels. Gower was behind the counter, with a crisp white pharmacist's jacket over his shirt and tie. His hand shook as he gave me my change. He had clean, clipped nails. Each one showed a half-moon.

"Got anything for a hangover?" I said.

"Just the thing, young man." He bent down and rummaged around beneath the counter. "Mr. Incles, isn't it?"

Above him, on the highest shelf, was as sweet and full a line-up of rye and scotch as I had ever seen. He had reordered since Christmas. On the shelves below, there were rows of apothecary jars mixed in with bottles of candy. Some jars were labeled and some weren't. I was right. This place could be a regular narcotics factory if he wanted. Or if anybody else wanted. I thought of George's glittery black eyes. It was still the kind of set-up where a mistake could happen very easily. Except from somebody's own particular point of view it might not be a mistake at all.

Gower emerged with a small yellow box. "Take one every two hours. As the box directs." He put the box on the counter.

"I suppose I could try not drinking," I said. "You ever try that?"

Gower drew himself up stiffly. "That would be effective too, sir. A preventative approach."

"Effective. But not profitable. For a man in your line of work."

Gower's frown deepened. The bell on the door tinkled, and a gaggle of school kids took over the front of the shop. They were screaming about ice cream and snapping on paper party hats. One of the kids had a red balloon on a string. The kids sat down in a row at the counter and bobbed around in place.

"Cute," I said. "Get them started young."

Over the row of pointy hats, Gower looked at me. I thought he might say something but he didn't. He watched me as I left, and he was not smiling. I was having that effect on a number of people in Bedford Falls.

I got in my car, and patted the pint of rye in my pocket. I figured I might have a long wait ahead and wanted to keep my energy up. I drove past Violet's Beautee Shoppe. It was a narrow shop front with purple and pink awnings. The windows were plastered with pictures of dames with a far away look in their eyes, as if they were listening to you talk love to them while they thought about this week's grocery shopping. I drove a few lots down, and parked outside the butcher shop. The beauty shop was in full view.

Violet did quite a bit of business. Women, old and young, went in and came out looking a lot more curly. They held their necks straight, and studied their reflections in the shop front windows. But not all Violet's customers were women. At quarter to four, a man in a dark hat and coat entered the shop with a swagger. It was Harry Bailey. I sat up and waited to see what would happen. He emerged about twenty minutes later. He stood on the sidewalk, with his hat still in his hands. His hair and the tops of his ears gleamed with brilliantine. So far, that was my day's big scoop: Harry Bailey had gotten a haircut. He ran his hand through his hair and put his hat on.

I lit a cigarette. Another half an hour went by. It got dark. Fewer people were going into Violet's shop. The lights dimmed. At five sharp, Violet came out on the sidewalk, and rolled up the awning.

A man passed by on the sidewalk, and stopped to talk to her a minute. She smiled and nodded and went back into the shop. A few minutes later she emerged with her hat and coat on.

I had wasted the afternoon finding out that Harry Bailey got his hair cut at Violet Bick's. Just then a car pulled up to the beauty shop and Violet Bick got in. Ernie was at the wheel. He smiled more broadly than business etiquette requires, and he wasn't wearing his cabbie cap. As he drove past, he turned his head. He smiled and waved at me, as though he had nothing to hide, as though his wife would understand perfectly why he was picking up Violet Bick when he was off-duty, and grinning like the big bad wolf the whole time he did it.

I thought some more. I went into the phone booth by Gower's drug store, and looked up Henry Potter's residence. "Potter, H.F." lived on Potter Road. For fun, I dialed Potter's number. No answer. I went back to Gower's and bought a flashlight. Gower pretended not to remember me. Then I made a dash for the butcher shop, and bought a pound of ground chuck.

CHAPTER SEVENTEEN

Potter's Road was a narrow, hilly lane that bordered Potter's Field on the north side. The field was scattered with deserted broken-down shacks that pocked the landscape like a crop of frozen tubers. I followed the road a mile or two, passed over the railroad tracks and drove another three minutes. By then, I could make out the outline of a hulking mansion up ahead.

I dimmed my lights and approached more slowly. A spiked iron fence surrounded the house. It was festooned with "Keep Out" and "Beware of the Dog" signs. On the right, beyond the fence, there was a garage, with its doors latched shut. Beside it, a few bare tree branches shook in the winter wind. Dogs were barking from the direction of the house.

I pulled the car over to the side of road, and parked behind a thick grove of pines. I went on foot towards the left side of the house. I looked at the fence and thought of climbing it but I didn't feel like being impaled that night. I walked around to the back of the house, following the fence, when my ankle gave way with a sharp twist. I looked down. At the base of the fence, a deep hollow had been dug out of the dirt. Maybe before the hard frost, one of Potter's dogs had been digging an escape route out of the place. For me it was a way in. I bundled my coat around me, and rolled like an armadillo into Potter's back yard.

Just inside the door, the dogs were barking. There were at least two of them. I went to the side of the house nearest the garage. The house was completely dark. There was a pair of windows above my shoulder. I used my hat for a glove and smashed the glass. Then I hoisted myself on to the ledge, and jumped off it, into the house of Henry Potter.

The room was large and high-ceilinged. I snapped on the flashlight. An oriental rug covered the whole of the floor. The room adjoined a smaller one, which contained an armchair and a side table with a telephone and a lamp. One end of this bigger room was taken up by a sprawling desk with a few papers on it. Beside the desk was a fireplace and a long marble mantelpiece. The mantelpiece held a police-line-up of a few massive clocks, but none of them looked to have been wound recently. The windows were covered with dark heavy drapes. The scratching of the dogs's nails and the pant of their hot breath came closer. I killed the flashlight and put it inside my coat. I opened a side door. It led into a small hallway. I heard growling. The dogs were hot-footing it down the hallway towards me. I supposed there might be nastier dogs than the ones Potter would keep, but not this side of Hades.

I unwrapped the meat, and held it out from me at arms length. The dogs rushed around the corner into the room. They were black with golden muzzles and stiff docked tails. Their eyes caught red from what little light there was. They looked at me, and before they could launch themselves at me, I clucked reassuringly and pitched the meat in back of them, into the hallway. They looked at each other, confused. My neck muscles tensed. The dogs turned abruptly, and went after the hamburger. I stuffed the paper wrapping into my pocket and shut the door against them.

I took the flashlight out and switched it on again. A

portrait of Potter hung above the fireplace. The room bore the same decorative touches as Potter's office in the bank. A globe of the world rested on a pedestal beside the fireplace. A bust of Napoleon brooded over it.

Just above Napoleon, on the wall, hung a framed front page. The Bedford Falls Sentinel, November 18, 1932. The headline read, "Potter Bails Out Local Bank." There was a smaller story on the far column, about the former bank head Joseph Enright, and how he had declared bankruptcy after Henry Potter called in his loan. On the wall beside the fireplace hung a framed letter. It was signed by Colonel Waldgreave, whoever he was, on December 4, 1944. It thanked Potter for serving as head of the local draft board. It looked like you could always count on Potter to do some sucker in. A standing lamp, with a heavily carved rosewood post and a dark green tasseled shade at its top, arched over the other side of the fireplace.

I tiptoed over to the desk, and sifted through the papers left out on it. A recent Bedford Falls Sentinel was on top. "President Decorates Harry Bailey," the headline read. On the green desk blotter, there was a receipt from Kepner's World Luggage store on Washington Street. It read "$2.10 - rprs," and was dated December 21. A watch chain was coiled up on one side of receipt, and beside it, a cigar lighter, embellished with a miniature human skull made of dark metal. Halfway hidden under the blotter, someone had stashed a manila file. I pulled it out. In neat copperplate, it was labeled: "Loans, Outstanding." I began leafing through it. A few names caught my eye: Ernie Bishop, Ellie Parker. Tom Partridge. And Violet Bick.

I was just settling down for a few hours pleasant reading on a cold winter's night when from the small side room, the phone rang.

CHAPTER EIGHTEEN

The phone rang six times and stopped. I wondered who would be ringing Potter's number besides me. I waited as the sound of the last ring became an echo.

Light streamed through the window behind me. I looked out the window and saw a car heading up the driveway. It was a dark, solid looking car that in a pinch could do the business of a hearse. A tall man in a dark coat and narrow-brimmed hat got out. His white shirtfront glittered in the dark. It was Whittier. He went around to the back of the house. The back door creaked as he opened it. I tried to breathe less loudly and I stayed put.

Whittier was whistling a happy little tune. A refrigerator door slammed shut. The dogs pattered off in the direction of Whittier's voice and the refrigerator.

"There you go, boys," Whittier said. He set something metal down on the floor. "What's the matter? Not hungry?"

Whittier's footsteps, lighter than I would have expected them to be on his own time, came along the hallway. He went into the smaller room directly across from me. He was nicely framed in the door jamb. He sunk into the armchair, and flicked on the lamp. He checked his watch.

Then he rubbed his nails against his lapel and held them to the lamplight. He examined them critically, with a sour little frown. He looked at his watch again.

The phone rang.

"Potter's residence," he answered in a butler's voice.

"Oh babe, in a manner of speaking," he said, in an entirely different voice. This voice had its tie off, its feet on the desk, and a snifter of brandy in its hand. "No. I just got here. Traffic was bad, that's all." There was a pause. "You're understanding. A cut above most dames, that's for sure." He laughed. His white teeth showed up against the yellowish tone to his skin. Seeing Whittier like this was like watching a wax figure come to life. It was fascinating but uncomfortable. Especially if you were holed up a few yards away from him in a house where you weren't wanted. He laughed. Then there was another pause.

"Stay sweet, sugar," he said. "But only for me." He hung up.

He closed his eyes and touched his fingertips to his temples. I bundled the manila file inside my coat. I left the way I came in, only this time I had no hamburger meat. From inside the house, the dogs were already kicking up a fuss again.

CHAPTER NINETEEN

I drove into Washington Street and parked under a streetlamp. Except for a few people going into Martini's, the street was empty. Rain fell in icy bullet-like drops, any one of which could have downed a hard-plated beetle. I pulled the file out from my coat and opened it. According to his loan application, Ernie Bishop was a licensed cab driver and mechanic. His business and personal address were the same, 28 Jefferson Avenue. He had taken out a three-year loan on March 27, 1945 for three hundred dollars. He had not given a reason for the loan on the application. About five months ago, Ernie Bishop started falling behind on his payments, a few days at first, and then a week at a time. Blond hair like Violet's must be pretty hard on the upkeep. It wasn't clear from this file what Potter intended to do about Ernie Bishop. Maybe Ernie could shed some light.

Mrs. Parker had taken out a two hundred dollar loan on December 20, 1944, for "Household expenses," a nice general category. Under it, she had penciled in "broken faucet - rust stains on carpet. Kitchen stove. Furnace." The past month, Mrs. Parker had missed her payment altogether. Again there was no indication of just what

Potter had in mind. I put her application back.

A yellowed press clipping fluttered out. I picked it up and pressed it flat. The paper was brittle and the name of the newspaper had broken off. The story was dated June 14, 1942. It was a report about an investigation into the jail system in Middlesex County, Massachusetts. The item included a picture of Michael Morrisey, the embattled police commissioner fighting for his job. He looked like a paper-thin slice of roast beef waiting for the gravy to be slopped over him, but maybe the light was bad.

According to the story, the investigation had been called after the escape of Clement Walters from the Charles Street jail. Walters had been the strong man in a bad checks scheme which had defrauded banks up and down the northeast coast of several thousand dollars. Walters had turned state's evidence, but he escaped before actually giving testimony, and Morrisey was in the soup.

I looked at the clipping. So far as I knew, Potter had no ties to Massachusetts. Maybe he was interested in the story because he ran a bank in the northeast and would want to know if any chiselers, other than himself, were abroad in the land. I wished Walters and Potter had met up, and I wondered how Morrisey made out, but only briefly. They weren't paying my bills. This clipping didn't seem to belong with the rest of the file, which were all bank loans. I stashed the clipping back into the file, and went on through the loan applications.

Tom Partridge had fallen two months behind on a seven hundred dollar loan he had taken out on June 7, 1945, for "general repairs." Violet Bick had taken out a one thousand dollar loan in 1943, according to the application: "to start a business - beauty salon." Her handwriting was thin, clear and slanted. Violet Bick had five years to pay the loan back. Her payments were all there and on time, and it was hard to see why her application was in this file at all. Maybe it was there to keep Ernie's application company. Maybe Potter knew something about them.

I lit a cigarette. At the very least, three of them had businesses and property that Potter may have wanted to snap up for himself. Those three would want Potter out of their hair, maybe even more than George Bailey did.

I started the car, and drove down Washington Avenue. I turned right onto Genesee Avenue, drove a block and then turned another right onto Monroe. The rain was battering onto the windshield. I turned on the wipers but the street only went more blurry. I passed a sign for Bedford Falls High School. The school building was set away from the street by a broad grassy front that at present was a field of stubble brown and dirty ice. Dead center in front of the school building, a car was parked. I'd seen it before: it was Whittier's.

I drove back around the block, and pulled over a few hundred yards behind Whittier's car. No one was in it. The street was dark and quiet. It was lined with modest houses with white fences and tidy front yards. I pulled my collar up and my hat down and got out of the car.

A few feet ahead, a frozen weeping willow swayed. I stationed myself under its thin wet branches. They brushed against my face, as taunting as a memory. Whittier was standing inside the high school, by a door. His back was facing me. He looked to be talking to someone I couldn't see. Then he pulled up his collar and put his hands in his coat pockets. He began walking towards the sidewalk, and I shrunk back into the shadows of the willow. Someone was walking beside him, someone I couldn't see except for the flash of the legs and the thickish high heels of the shoes. Someone was also laughing, a light, high, tinkling laugh that was totally without mirth. Someone was a woman. That was as much as I could make out.

They both got into Whittier's car. The car drove off, turned left at the end of the road, and then was lost to the streets of Bedford Falls.

CHAPTER TWENTY

The next morning broke drizzling and gray. I washed, shaved and dressed. I was thinking about the flapjacks over at TipTop and the magenta-nailed waitress, when there was a knock at my door. Without waiting, Mrs. Parker walked in.

"It was good five minutes since you had the hot water running so I figured you'd be decent by now," she said. She was looking over my head and all around my torso to take in as much as she could of the room. "You're careful to turn that water off properly, aren't you?"

"Yes, ma'am," I said. "We don't want the faucet running and the carpet getting touched up with rust stains."

She gave me a sharp look. "No, I don't. I just wanted to be sure you got whatever it was that young woman had for you the other day. I hope you didn't mind my letting her in."

"Oh, I got it all right." I grinned. "She was okay. Until she tried to convert me to Mormonism."

"Violet Bick is no Mormon. Unless these days they have it so it's the woman what gets to have a lot of husbands." Mrs. Parker's eyes had completed their search as far as the closet door. Now they started in the other direction. She looked at me and drew her afghan closer around her. "Any news on George Bailey?"

I straightened my back and looked at my feet, as though I were an administrator of the law, sworn to secrecy and correct as can be. She bought it and sighed.

"The week's rent," she said. "You will be able to pay it?"

I reached for my coat, fished around the pocket, and counted out twelve one dollar bills. "Cancel all your debts, Mrs. Parker."

She didn't bat an eyelash. She'd spied something. She plucked the white butcher's paper out of my coat pocket. She held it, crumpled, in her hand. She looked at it and then at me. "Now, young man, you do realize there is no cooking on the premises. I don't want you in the kitchen, underfoot and dirtying up the sink. I can't have it."

"I understand." I reached for my coat. "It must be pretty hard, running a business like this. Keeping everything in repair."

"Not as hard as some businesses I can think of." She turned to leave. "I expect you'll probably be hearing from George Bailey." She was already heading down the stairs. "Now that he's been released and all."

That's what I like, a client who keeps me informed. I went out and stopped at the TipTop. I was finishing my home fries when Ernie Bishop came in. He pushed his cabbie hat back from his forehead and sat down at the counter.

"Morning, Betty. Coffee and toast. And eggs and bacon too if you don't mind."

"You're looking pretty chipper," she said.

"I'm feeling pretty chipper."

I went up to the counter to pay my bill. "Hello, Ernie."

"Mr. Incles! How's the car running?"

"Pretty well. Of course, I don't put it through the kind of paces you do. Stop and start. Picking people up and dropping them off, till all hours of the night. I bet that takes a lot out of a motor, even one with plenty of horsepower."

"Oh, I don't know." His back stiffened.

"Not to mention a marriage."

"Huh?"

I cocked my head to one side. "Talked to Bert lately?"

Ernie turned slightly paler. "Yeah. So what?"

"Any tips I'd want to know about?"

"Depends. What stakes you playing for?"

"Pretty high. Like maybe a new word on Potter's cause of death. Maybe something else."

"I already told you, mister. He choked on his own money. That's no secret."

"That's official?"

"Not only that. It's obvious." The waitress put a full plate in front of him and he started into it.

"As obvious as a blonde getting into the backseat of an off-duty taxi, I bet," I said.

"Yeah," Ernie took a gulp of coffee, and perked up. "I bet too." He winked. "I'll keep you in mind next time I talk to Bert. Can't say when that will be."

"I'd appreciate that," I said.

I left the TipTop, and crossed the street to the Building and Loan. I had to field a long flight of steep stairs up to the office. George Bailey was standing behind a desk, counting quarters and dimes.

"I thought you'd had enough of that stuff," I said. "Filthy lucre."

He seemed delighted to see me. He took my hand and pumped it up and down as though it was Standard Oil's main rig. "Isn't it wonderful! I've been released."

"For now," I said.

"This may be the end of our professional relationship."` He gave me a wild grin. "What do you know about that?" Then he started shaking my hand again.

"I wouldn't count on it," I said.

"How's that?"

"A few things are cleared up. About the eight thousand, you didn't lose it. Uncle Billy did. He pretty much let that drop when I met him the other day at Martini's. No wonder he doesn't carry cash anymore."

George blinked and took a step back. "Don't tell anyone. It would destroy Uncle Billy. Me, well, I can handle that kind of heat."

I wasn't so sure but I went on. "Somewhere along the line, Potter got hold of the money. My guess is that Potter got Billy rattled, that he threatened him into handing over the money, I'm not sure with what. Potter probably had the whole thing planned so the money would go missing the day the bank examiner was in town. When Potter was killed, he was entering the eight thousand into his own books." I paused. "It could be whoever did him in was angry about that money and had plenty of reason to be."

"Now hold on, mister. Just a durned minute," George said. "You're not saying Uncle Billy did it? You can't think that."

"No, I don't. But Callaghan might. Or he might think you set him up to do it."

"Well, so long as we stick to the truth, we'll be fine," George said. He spoke with a slight stutter. His head nodded up and down.

He was coming from left field again. I winced at the word "truth" as though I had sunk my teeth into a lemon. So far, truth was our biggest problem.

"Truth doesn't have much to do with a lawman's case, Mr. Bailey. The question is evidence. Callaghan obviously couldn't find enough on you. Yet. But he'll keep digging. And if he can't find enough on you, he'll start looking at your family and friends. And there he'll probably find it. For your sake, I hope he does."

I looked around me. It was easy to see why an ambitious young man would have wanted out of this place. The Building and Loan was dusty and sad. The main desk was rickety and sagged under the weight of an ancient typewriter. The other desk tops were cluttered with staplers, pens, erasers, and paper clips. The leg of one desk was propped up on a yellowing phone directory. A floor plank underneath my foot was coming loose.

"Let's sit down in my office," George said. He opened a smudged-up glass door, and quickly moved some papers from his chair to the floor. I sat down on a wooden chair facing his desk. I looked out a moment through the window in back of him. Butchers were still selling pork chops and druggists were peddling aspirin and soda pop. The clock in his outer office struck ten.

"Mr. Bailey, you're a lucky man in a lot of ways," I said. "Your friends would do anything for you. Bail you out, like they did on Christmas Eve. That's the problem I'm having. One of your friends has offered to give you an alibi and nothing checks out."

"What do you mean, give me an alibi?"

"Say they were with you all night, when they weren't."

"Martini!" George said. "That old son of a gun! Now don't get mad with him, Mr. Incles. I was at his place Christmas Eve. He just figures he'll be a little fuzzy about the exact times."

"It wasn't Martini I was referring to."

"Well, Bert then," he said. He was a lot less certain. "Or Ernie maybe."

I pulled out my pack of cigarettes. I had sat on them. "It was Violet Bick."

"Well, now Violet Bick..." He waved his arms around. Then they went still.

I regarded a squashed cigarette. "Just how close are you and Miss Bick?"

"Good friends, that's all." George raked a hand through his hair. "I know what you've heard. That I was sweet on her and giving her money. Well, I'm not, but I did, on Christmas Eve. Violet came here that night. She was desperate. She told me she needed money to get of town, to start again someplace else, New York City I think. I gave her a few twenties for food and rent. But it was my own money. You can check that."

"And you think that's why she's willing to lie for you?"

"Yes, sir, I do. I tried to help and I didn't ask a lot of questions," George said. "You'll find that goes down pretty well around here."

"I'll try to remember that. Why'd she change her mind about leaving?"

"I don't know," George put his face in his hands. "She never told me. Come to think of it, she never told me why she had to leave town in such a hurry either."

"And you never asked?"

"Like I said - "

The door opened, and Harry Bailey sauntered in, confident, as if he owned the place.

"Oh sorry George," Harry said. "I didn't think you were still here. I'd have knocked."

"Harry, this -" George began.

"We've met," Harry said.

"I was just on my way out." I stood up.

"It's a good thing George has the kind of friends who'll see him out of trouble," Harry said. "I got to them all, before Callaghan could. He'll have trouble getting two words out of them. That's the kind of loyalty you can't buy."

"No, you can't. Certainly not for twenty-five dollars a day, plus expenses. Not even if you throw in eight cents a mile for the car."

Harry lips curled. "You know what they say: blood is thicker than water."

"And I'll let you know what I say: bloodshed is thicker than either of them. You'd know that if you were in my business. But I forgot. You've only seen the kind of killing a man can get a medal for. Except around here, you'd almost expect to get a medal for killing Potter, wouldn't you? Or did the one you snagged in Washington cover everything?"

"I've got a good mind -" Harry said. He made a fist.

"You're sure of that?"

George stood up. "Now fellas -"

"Don't like it, little brother?" I said. "Just a sample of what Callaghan's going to try now that he's had to release his chief suspect. And I'd watch those late afternoon appointments with Violet Bick if I were you. That ring's not just for show - you are married, aren't you? People might get the wrong idea."

I walked out and whistled loudly all the way down the staircase. When I gained the street, I headed over to Gower's. The old man was in his back office but he straightened up his tie when he saw me coming. I went into the public phone box and placed a call to a buddy of mine in the Albany DA's office. After we finished wisecracking each other, I got to business.

"This is a long shot, but I need whatever you can dig up on a Michael Morrisey. He was Police Commissioner in Boston a few years back. He got into trouble the summer of 1942. That was when a fellow called Clement Walters went AWOL. Walters was part of a bad checks scheme, and was slated to spill his guts on behalf of the state. Only he busted out of the jail instead, and decided not to come back. Maybe the coffee was lousy. Anyway, last I heard, Morrisey was getting slammed in the press pretty hard."

"Morrisey?" he said. I spelled out the name.

"When you find anything out, send it along, pronto." He took down my address. Something like static started playing up on the phone line. "I've got a bad connection," I said. "Oh, and Mrs. Parker? Don't wait up tonight. I'll be late coming in."

The man in Albany laughed. "Sure thing," he said. We rang off.

At the corner newsstand, I picked up a paper. I pushed my hat around on my head and laughed. A redhead passed me and gave the kind of look that's supposed to make you lie down in her path and wave your arms and legs, frantic as a bug on its back. I tipped my hat to her and grinned. I leaned against the brick wall. In five-point type, the motive I'd been looking for was staring me smack in the face.

CHAPTER TWENTY-ONE

"Potter's Heir is Longtime Assn't." screamed a headline. I folded the paper in half, thereby muffling the headline's scream about fifty per cent. Henry Potter, local business man and president of Bedford Falls Savings and Trust, named as sole heir to his estate his longtime assistant Charles Gordon Whittier, it was revealed today. The estate was valued in the range of $375,000. A memorial service for Mr. Potter, who died suddenly on Christmas Eve, will be held at eleven o'clock today at the First Methodist Chapel. "Died suddenly": a nice touch. I pulled out one of my squashed cigarettes and stood on the street corner having a smoke. It was the most fun I ever looked forward to having in a church.

The First Methodist Church was a square wooden building behind the bank. The bank cast a long cold shadow over it. I checked my watch. It was five past eleven. I hurried up the three small stone steps into an unadorned room lined with empty pews. An organ played somewhere above me. Slow, heavy gray notes filled the air. It was as if Methodist heaven and a hangover had collided. I sat in the back pew and waited. Mr. Gower entered, silent and tight-lipped. He had his white druggist's coat folded over his arm. He looked as vivacious as a cigar store Indian. He sat down in a pew close to the front. He hadn't noticed me.

A middle-aged man, his face mottled red from the cold, bustled in. He had wire-rimmed glasses that glittered on his face like twin patches of ice. I figured him for Potter's lawyer. He checked the time on his pocket watch and sat four pews ahead of me.

Violet Bick arrived. She was wearing a nubbly light green suit with pale lavender and pink trimming. She looked like the longest, curviest stalk of asparagus I had ever seen. It made me want to eat up all my vegetables like mother told me. Violet took a frilly handkerchief from her handbag and daubed at her eyes. She looked at me as she did it. Then she sat down beside the man in the glasses. He had to move in, but when he turned and saw Violet he decided he didn't mind.

Whittier came into the church, with the air of one bestowing himself. He wore a black coat and a squared-off black derby. His face was stern and his lips looked bloodless. He sat close to the front, near Gower. He didn't acknowledge anyone. He'd come here to count his blessings, all 375,000 of them.

It was almost quarter past when George Bailey entered the church, his head bowed. Harry and Mary Bailey followed, with Mrs. Hatch between them. An older woman followed. She had the same lanky cast to her face as George, and I guessed was his mother. Their faces were stiff. Harry wore his officer's uniform. Uncle Billy scuttled in last on his short, stocky legs. The Bailey contingent crowded into the pew just ahead of Violet and the lawyer. George and Mary acknowledged Violet with a jerky nod apiece. The organ went on playing. The notes slowed and thickened, and then they stopped.

Bert and Ernie came in together. They sat just ahead of me. Bert took off his cap, and held it in his hands. He gestured at Ernie to do the same. Ernie looked confused

E. N. McMAHON

and Bert lost patience and reached over and did it for him. From a side door up front, the minister entered the pulpit. He had steely white hair and a comfortable gut. He straightened his stiff collar with a broad pinkish hand. He looked like he figured you could be a Christian without losing any sleep over it.

"Good friends," he intoned. "We gather together this morning to mark the loss of Henry Potter. But let us think first not of his death but of his life. For Henry Potter was a man who understood many things. His interests were wide and -"

"I'll say. Interests in the department stores, the bus routes, the bank, even the Building and Loan," Ernie said under his breath. Bert started to laugh. Then he remembered where he was. He frowned and looked straight ahead.

"Henry Potter was a man who understood the final accounting," the minister went on. "That is the accounting we will all someday face. What is in the balance is our souls. What is in our interest is to save them. Invest them wisely. Take stock - "

Bert nudged Ernie at this point and rolled his eyes.

" - all the natural good God has to offer, and give Him no just claim against your soul."

"The gas bill came due yesterday," Billy said in a loud whisper. Mary tried to keep him quiet. "I just remembered. I'll find it, Mary. Nothing to worry about." His eyes were round with fear. He rummaged through his pockets and found nothing but a handkerchief. He turned his straw hat over and over in his hands. He looked at Violet. He put his fingers to his lips. "Shh," he said. Then he rose and hurried out of the church. The rest of the Baileys bobbed around for a moment but they stayed put.

"In these days, the first days of light after so many dark days of war, a shadow is still cast over us," the minister said. "Many young men have fallen in foreign lands, never to see home again. But that shadow is lifting. Be joyous

80

then."

Mrs. Hatch burst into tears. Mary touched a hand to her mother's shoulder. Violet began sniffling. In a minute, all three were bawling.

"Be joyous then I say," the minister boomed. "Henry Potter has gone to rest in the town of his birth. He was called to His Maker in the winter of his life, but still too soon for our understanding. The ways of the Lord indeed are strange."

George Bailey and Gower lowered their chins.

"Henry Potter's ledger is forever closed. May God grant that each of us ends our days with our books in such inestimable order."

"And fleshed out with a cool eight grand," Ernie said under his breath. Bert took a swipe at him.

The organ started playing again. The heavy gray notes filled the air. Gower filed out first. He nodded at George with a slight smile. Bert and Ernie stood up to leave.

"Hey, Mr. Incles!" Bert said. "I didn't recognize you out of custody." Ernie smiled and avoided my eyes.

I raised three fingers in a weary salute.

Violet Bick and the lawyer headed out. I turned to watch them. He said a few words to her on the church steps. He moved on. She waited. The Baileys filed out. George looked pretty rough, like he was seasick. The Baileys walked past Violet Bick. Harry nodded without a smile. Whittier got up and left the church. He stopped a moment at the steps and straightened his hat. Violet looked at him. She didn't say anything. She didn't have to. She plucked a bit of lint from his sleeve and smiled. Then she headed down the street. Whittier waited a moment. He went off in the opposite direction.

I went out on the steps and took out another squashed cigarette. Between Violet Bick's decision to leave town and her decision to stay, one thing had changed: Potter had been murdered. Whittier gained big by that death, it turned out. And what I had just seen made everything fall into place. Violet was Whittier's sweetie. She was one who phoned Whittier the night I was at Potter's, and owned the pair of legs I glimpsed by the high school gym. Whatever footsie she might have going with Ernie, a cabman's salary couldn't compete with Potter's stash.

And one other thing was clear: I was overdue for a haircut.

CHAPTER TWENTY-TWO

Violet's Beautee Shoppe was empty. The bell on the door rattled as I came in. The place was small and smelled of ammonia and hairspray and vain aspirations. Violet emerged from the back room. She was wearing a peach-colored smock over her dress. She was set to smile a welcome, but when she saw it was me, her face went blank.

"Can I help you?" she said.

"I'd like a haircut."

"Have an appointment?"

"Do I need one?"

She drew in her breath. "Any style in mind?"

"Shorter. Just be sure to leave my head attached to my neck."

She smiled. "Okay, Mr. Incles. Truce."

She wrapped a thick towel around my neck and sat me in a chair that backed into a sink. She lathered my hair and rinsed it out with warm water. Violet smiled down at me. I thought I was dreaming, or in heaven. Then she turned the water off.

"All set," she said. "Step this way."

I sat down in front of a triangle-shaped mirror. She combed my hair with her fingers. She looked over a line-up of razors and picked one up.

"It must be quite an undertaking, getting a place like this started," I said.

"I'll say. It's not easy for a girl on her own to open an account and arrange for credit."

"Say, you must be a minister," I said.

She laughed. "He was something, all right." She cut my hair with close even snips.

"So was Potter. You must have had to go to Potter yourself. To get a loan, I mean."

She stopped cutting and her eyes looked at my eyes in the mirror. "Everyone in town had to turn to Potter if they wanted a bank loan." Then she went back to cutting, with sharper and faster snips. I watched her reflection.

"But after all your work getting this place started, you were thinking of leaving town. Why?"

"Just a mixed up kid, I guess," she said.

"Why did you change your mind?"

"A girl just does that kind of thing."

"What else does a girl do, Miss Bick?"

She stopped cutting. "I don't know what you mean."

"Come on. Potter had something on you. What was it?"

"I don't know what you're - "

"Christmas Eve, you were all set to leave. And then you changed your mind. What changed your mind was Potter's murder. You know George Bailey didn't do it because you know who did do it."

Violet was holding the razor to the back of my neck. I watched her in the mirror. She wasn't looking at my reflection in the mirror anymore. She was looking at me directly, and with something more than anger.

"And you decided you could stay after all because you knew Potter would be dead," I said. "Because you're the one who killed him."

Her hands relaxed. She gave a short laugh. "You've been working too hard, mister."

84

The phone at the front of the shop rang.

"Excuse me," she said.

It was a hurried, under-the-breath conversation.

"Yeah." Violet twisted the phone cord on her little finger. "The usual place. Eight's fine." She hung up.

She combed my hair into place. She eased a brushful of oily stuff through it. She stood back from the chair and regarded her work critically. "How 'bout a shave?"

"No, thanks, sister. One brush with a razor is my daily limit." She was a cool number, but she had let a lot fall, and I didn't mean my hair clippings. She knew who did it. And so did I.

I went to the front of the shop to pay the bill. An old-fashioned register took up most of the counter space. Beside it, there was a display full of plastic pocket combs, brown and black.

"I'll take one of those," I said.

"That'll be another five cents." She took a tiny key out of her pocket and opened the register. She counted my change out of the drawer. "Need a bag?"

"Just a receipt."

"A receipt?" Her lips made a thin coral-tinted line. "For a five-cent comb?"

"And the haircut. If you don't mind."

She drew in her breath, as if she would bust a gut. "I'll have to write one out by hand."

"That's okay."

She looked around, found a scrap of paper, and wrote out a bill. Then she pushed it to me with the tip of her index finger. She turned and went into the back room of the shop.

I headed over to Martini's for a steak. Then I went home to wash the stuff out of my hair. I had a date lined up that night myself, once I trailed Whittier to the "usual place."

CHAPTER TWENTY-THREE

I headed out just after seven. Mrs. Parker was nowhere to be heard. A cold wet rain was falling. The roads were slick, and the white light from my headlights bounced off them.

The way to Potter's house was longer than I remembered. I passed by the field scattered with deserted shacks. I followed the road past the railroad tracks and drove another five minutes, until I saw the outline of the massive house up ahead. I killed the lights and parked in the shadow of the pine trees. I headed up on foot. Potter's house was dark. I beamed the flashlight a second and saw the driveway was empty. Somewhere further inside, the dogs growled. Whittier wasn't home.

I got back in the car and took a swig. I could wait there, but I didn't see much use in that. Violet Bick struck me as the kind of girl who expected a lot more than a cozy night at home. I started back into town. I turned right on Monroe. I was passing by the high school when I caught sight of something that made me slow down and pull over. It would have made me clap my hands in delight, if I were the clapping type. Whittier's car was parked by the side of road. I checked my watch, seven thirty, not even much of a wait. It was getting to be my lucky day. I drove around the block and parked a few hundred yards behind his car.

Big rain drops fell onto the icy brown stretch of ground in front of the high school and bounced back as high as the fire hydrant. I sat in my car, waiting. I had a bottle of whiskey beside me to keep me warm. It was doing a pretty good job.

A kid in a stocking cap was out walking his dog, a nippy yippy little number the type Chinese emperors used to keep swallowed up in their sleeves. The kid tugged the dog along on a leash. The dog stopped by the left front wheel of my car. It had confused the car with the hydrant. I looked at the kid. He was looking at his dog and tugging it in the opposite direction. I lit up a cigarette. The kid and his dog moved on.

A red Ford passed me. A woman came walking down the street, with little mincing steps as if a shoe shop clerk had persuaded her to buy a pair of heels a half-size too small. I sat up straight. She was bundled up to the hilt and then some. A thick knitted scarf was wound around her neck, and reached well beyond the level of her chin up to her mouth. Her hair was covered by a wide-brimmed hat that held onto to her head like an uncompromising green-felt horizon. She kept her head down, out of the rain.

I watched her come closer to my car. I waited as she passed it. I had my hand on the door handle to make a break for it as she walked towards the school. She walked right past it. She went a few lots further, and then turned left into a path lined with hedges.

I looked at my watch. It was quarter to eight. I screwed the top off the bottle and took a swig. The bottle top rolled of the seat to the floor of the car. I bent down to get it back and bumped my head on the steering wheel. Nothing ever goes as smoothly as it does in the pictures. I had my arm propped against the window and was rubbing my head, when a face swam out of the darkness in front of me. I jumped back, startled, and hit the horn by accident.

Ernie smiled at me through the glass. He was wearing his cabbie's cap.

"You okay there, Mr. Incles?"

I rolled down the window.

He poked his hand through, and I shook it. I was sorry I had forgotten my calling cards.

"Your car break down? Gee, I thought I'd given it a good going-over. You need any help? I can get you help. Matter of fact, I am the help." He pointed to a large jalopy across the road.

"No, thanks, bud." I said. "I'm okay. Just pulled over to get my bearings."

"I can give you directions. Set you up with a road map even." He went over to his cab.

I looked at my watch. It was five minutes to eight. I wondered what Ernie was up to out here this time of night.

He came back to my car. "Here you go, mister. Not that Bedford Falls is such a big city." He laughed loudly, a hee-hawing kind of laugh that sucks in all the free air it can get and then keels over without missing a beat.

I looked around. No one else was on the road. Perhaps they had been scared away by the commotion.

"You sure you're okay, Mr. Incles? I live just a few houses down. I'm headed there now. You want to come in and sit down or anything?"

"No, thanks." I held the map out to him.

"You keep that," he said. "I got plenty of them. Oh, by the way, I talked to Bert. Nothing today, but I'll keep you posted." He tipped his cap at me, and headed across the street. He drove off and honked as he went past.

This hicksville fellowship was getting on my nerves. It had ruined my stake-out. But maybe that's what Ernie had in mind.

It was eight o'clock. No sign of a car or a passerby. Fifteen minutes passed, then five more. Then it hit me. Maybe I'd been at Whittier's and Violet's usual place this whole time. I got out of the car, shut the door, and headed towards the high school. The wide green door gave way easily. It turned on creaky hinges, and opened into a cavernous empty space.

It was the school gym. The hard wooden floor was well-polished, and at first my heels skidded on it. There was a low deep sound from inside the building, like a furnace or a motor turning. Silvery-white light, like light from a projection booth, filtered in from the street through a high square window above the basketball net. There was a roll of canvas piled up along the right-hand length of the gym. I decided I better walk on that.

I was moving across the gym towards the center. I heard a wheel and chain, cranking away somewhere below. By now I could see the floor had opened up ahead of me, and given way to a swimming pool underneath. The watery gap in the floor widened aseveral inches. The motor gave a lurch, and stopped. Just the typical high school gym-and-pool arrangement you'd expect to find in this screwball town. I could have jumped in. That would have made two bodies in the water.

But only one of them would have been alive

CHAPTER TWENTY-FOUR

A large dark shape was floating in the pool, like a shadow of something hovering far above. The shape turned over lazily. The face was as white as the belly of a beached perch, and there was a large purple gash on the left temple. Whittier was dead. His derby bobbed along the surface of the water. His gal had arrived and left early, by the look of things. Not a neon blonde in the place.

I stepped carefully along the floor in front of the water. I didn't know what I was looking for, but I was looking. On my fourth or fifth step, my foot hit something. I looked down. I had nearly hitched a ride on a pocket watch. I bent down, snapped it shut, and slipped it inside my coat. I headed towards the door. It was wide open, but not empty.

A tall broad shape was standing in it, as unyielding as an upright freezer chest.

"Who's there?" the freezer shape called out.

It was Bert the cop. When he saw it was me, he smiled his big grin. "Mr. Incles! What are you doing here? I just saw the door open as I was passing by and thought I better have a look-see. How'd the pool get opened out? You decide you wanted to swim a few laps?"

"No," I said. "But somebody else did. Or had it decided for him."

"Huh?" Bert came closer to the pool and looked in. He turned to face me. He was no longer smiling. "Mr. Incles, you're going to have to come with me." He shook his head. "You don't seem like a bad fellow. But whenever I run into you, it seems like somebody gets killed."

Callaghan was pretty jolly that evening. He sat across his desk from me and tried to suppress a grin. The lamp had a high watt bulb, and the neck was twisted around so that the light hit me smack in the eyes. He sat facing the wall and giving me his profile.

"You're a regular flying dutchman," Callaghan said. "You stay here much longer and the whole town will be wiped out." He laughed. I tried to move my head and get the light out of my eyes, but I couldn't so I gave up.

"Let me get this straight," Callaghan went on. "You were out looking for a liquor store that was still open, and you got lost. You pulled over by the school, you noticed the door was ajar and you decided to have a look."

"Right."

"And just a minute or two later, the police officer did the same thing."

"Check."

"You didn't see anything?"

"Just a dead body. Nothing special in Bedford Falls these days."

"Very funny." Callaghan turned and waved towards the hallway. "Wait out there with Bert. He'll keep an eye on you."

"What am I waiting for?"

"Me to decide what to do with you."

"Am I under suspicion?"

Callaghan grinned. "That depends on a number of things."

"Like what?"

"A particular report."

"By whom?"

"I've never liked twenty questions."

"Especially when somebody else is asking them," I said. "I got it in five."

Callaghan twisted around in his chair and gave me the benefit of his other profile. "Beat it."

I followed Bert into the hallway. It smelled of ammonia and carbon paper. We faced two closed doors. There was a sliver of light under the door on the right. Bert opened the door on the left, snapped on the light, and led me in. The room was small and cramped even though the only things in it were two chairs and a table with a couple of old National Geographics. Bert sat down, picked up one of the magazines and yawned. I sat down and just yawned.

"Now don't get yourself in a state," Bert said. "We're just waiting for the coroner to finish his preliminary report. I expect we'll be out in a jiff." He opened up the magazine and began flipping through it. Then he stopped and rubbed his nose with a flat hand. He looked over at me. "Well, I will be, anyway."

"Wonder what they'll find out."

"Never can tell. Now the one on Potter took some time but that was because Dr. Campbell was out of practice. We didn't have much call for autopsies, until you arrived. Not meaning no disrespect." He turned back to his magazine.

"Money really kill Potter?"

"All that was in that buzzard's body was a fistful of dollars and a grain or two of that drugstore medicine he always took. I'd say it was pretty clear. Hey, how 'bout that? It says here alligators in the Amazon grow to over twenty feet. I hear tell Whittier had a pretty long soak. About an hour or so before you found him."

"A little birdie told me you might have a tip or two," I said. I moved an inch closer to him and waited for him to go on.

"Huh?" Bert said. "What tip?"

"You know." I lowered my voice. "Ernie."

Bert's eyes widened like a pair of eggs cracking out of their nice tidy shells. "Can't talk about that in here, mister."

He clammed up like a canary with a sudden case of lock jaw, and went flipping through his magazine faster. But he had already let enough notes spill, and they put the time of Whittier's death between six-thirty and seven-thirty. That was worth knowing. I lit a cigarette and thought. Fifteen minutes passed. A door opened in the hallway, and the footsteps of two men went down the hallway. A few more minutes passed. There was a knock at the door. Bert went to answer it. Callaghan stood there grinning. He gestured Bert out of the room. Bert turned and nodded good night to me.

"Scram, amigo," Callaghan said.

"I'm not wanted on suspicion?" I stood up.

"Of what? Maybe it was an accident." Callaghan laughed and put his hands in his pockets. He was feeling pretty good. "I had this one down to two suspects. One of them is free tonight. One of them isn't."

"Who's the other lucky fellow?"

"You better mind your own business."

"Okay. Mind if I ask why I'm out of the running?"

Callaghan looked at me as though I were a telephone that was out of order when he needed to make an important call. He took a deep breath and decided to be patient. "Let's just say for the crucial time period your whereabouts are accounted for. I wondered why you happened to be by the high school in your car, I admit, but even you wouldn't be so stupid if you did have anything to do with it. I also have it on good authority that you were lost. Somehow I can believe that. At least for now." He bared his gumful of teeth. "Because George Bailey, well, he doesn't have a cat's whisker of a story." Callaghan took his hands out of his pockets. He hitched his thumbs through his suspenders. "A drop like this takes guts, I'll give him that much. First day he gets out, too. Killing Potter wasn't enough for him. He had to get Potter's goon, too." He would be telling this story in court soon and he was practicing to get it in shape. He looked at me sideways and gave me an icy, committed-cop's eye, as if I were in the jury box. "This vendetta ends here and now."

"That's all you've got on him?" I said. "A hunch?"

Callaghan sat down, took out a pen, and began doodling on the cover of a dead National Geographic.

"You know, Callaghan, I've got a right molar that acts up pretty good when it's going to rain, or the stock market's about to crash. Maybe you want to borrow it to prove Bailey's guilty. Or you could read a saucerful of tea leaves. And there's a butcher over on Central and I bet he'd give you a pile of chicken entrails to check out. The town sure is lucky that your methods are so advanced."

"Cut the cracks, wise-guy," Callaghan said. He put the pen down. "I cannot divulge official information. You may remember that from your days with the law. Let's just say we've been finding more holes in Bailey's Christmas Eve story than in a warehouse full of swiss cheese, and I'm including the rat-holes. The story he's got for tonight's even worse. His own wife can't vouch for him. And speaking of which, his friends, when they do try to help him, well, with friends like that - "

"Who needs alibis," I said.

Callaghan laughed. "Take a powder."

I headed out to my car and looked at my watch. Quarter to ten. Not too late to make a social call.

CHAPTER TWENTY-FIVE

I pulled over by a phone booth and made a run for it. I still got soaked. A "Bick, V." was listed on 154 Saxon Street. I got in the car and started driving. The glare from the street lights bounced off the slick black road. It was all I could do to see where I was going.

154 Saxon Street was a small brick apartment house with peeling white shutters and an attitude. "Saxon Gardens" a sign in Olde-English lettering announced. "No Salesmen Please." I huddled by the front door. Fifteen names were listed. None of other fourteen meant anything to me. I pressed a buzzer and waited. Minutes passed as they have a way of doing when I'm in a hurry. Then I was buzzed in, no questions asked.

Violet lived in room 8-D. It was on the second floor, the last apartment on the left. She was standing by the door when I got there. Her eyes were puffy as though she'd been crying and her hair could have used professional care.

"Come on in," she said. She used the same antifreeze I did. "Have a seat."

I sat down in an upholstered chair. Its pale blue cushioning rose up to surround me like a bad dream. I was sinking fast. She took the sofa. The lamp beside it had a fluted pink shade, and it cast a rosy false glow over her face. She slipped off her shoes and tucked her legs under her like a sorority sister settling in with a bowl of popcorn.

She turned towards me, out of the light. A slightly sticky smile spread across her face like a honey glaze, and then it hardened. "Now if you've come to return that haircut, I'm afraid that's just not possible," she said. "No siree."

"I have a receipt," I said.

She flushed. Then she remembered to grin. "I bet you do. But that don't make no never mind."

"What could I picture you giving a return on, Miss Bick?" I said. "A heart, maybe?"

"Only when it's broken beyond repair, Mr. Incles." A little meaningless chitchat would prime us both up like a straight shot of hooch, before we turned to business. She looked up with a sideways glance.

"When I came in, you seemed a little upset, Miss Bick. If you don't mind my saying."

She bit her lip. "I got stood up, is all." She tried smiling again. She was acting just the way a pretty girl who wasn't used to getting stood up, and was putting a brave face on it, would act - if she'd been studying for the part.

"I'm sure the fellow had a good reason," I said.

There was a small silence, about the size of bread box. We both contemplated it. Then I said, "Miss Bick, I have some bad news for you. I'm glad you're already sitting down. You can probably tell that I'm not good at creampuff phrases so I'll just have to say it. Charles Whittier is dead."

"Wh-what? Charlie?" Her face was frozen with disbelief. Or with something else that made her face look frozen. I let her sit for a minute while her face thawed out, and then it started churning. She stood up and went to the window. She clutched a length of curtain in her hands so hard that her knuckles turned white. "Oh no, oh no," she kept saying, in a voice as muted and regular as breathing. Then she let loose with a single loud sob. She stood there a while longer looking out at night in the treacherous burg, but not seeing a thing. After a while she left the window and sat down again. Her eyes were dry. For that I was grateful.

"No one knows exactly how it happened, but the police are hot and heavy on a suspect," I said.

She drew in her breath. "I wonder who. Why." She put her hands to her mouth and then let them sink slowly to the level of her knee.

"I'll tell you the truth, Miss Bick. I think you know a lot about this whole mess, and what you know concerns my client. You remember George Bailey, don't you? Now you and Whittier were good friends, better friends than many a husband and wife I know. I'm sorry I had to tell you the bad news. That is, if you didn't know it already."

Her jaw tightened. "You got a lot of nerve," she said. "Accusing me at work and then following me home to play the same stunt over again. As if I don't have enough to worry about. Don't you have anything better to do? If you have even a shred of evidence-"

"Why don't you call the police, Miss Bick, and tell them I'm harassing you? But you better remember what I can tell them about your eagerness to give false evidence. They may manufacture evidence themselves but they don't like it when amateurs go into the business."

She frowned but she shut up.

"What time did you go to the high school?" I said.

"I didn't go to any high school. What would I want at the high school?" She wasn't bad, for someone who was lying. She didn't stumble over the words and her nose didn't grow a perceptible fraction.

"Sometimes the usual place turns out to be fairly unusual. Don't mind me, Miss Bick. I was just testing the waters. Pooling our resources. Getting into the swim of things. If you know what I mean."

Her eyebrows jerked as though they were on strings and she managed to look bewildered. She was a smooth one, I had to give her that. She wasn't giving anything away, or even a hint that she had any merchandise. "Just what do you want from me, mister?" She settled back into the sofa and closed her eyes. "I've had a terrible night and I'd like to be left alone."

"Whittier's had an even more terrible night. So has George Bailey."

"Beat it, mister."

"You know we'll have to talk sooner or later," I said. "About Potter and Whittier and why you changed your mind on Christmas Eve."

She didn't move a muscle. "Scram or I start screaming."

I let myself out. Her hat was hanging on the back of the door. It still didn't like me any more than I liked it.

CHAPTER TWENTY-SIX

I got into my car and lit a cigarette. Violet Bick knew a lot more than she was saying, that much was sure. She was set to skip town and then she didn't. That was interesting. She was Whittier's girl and now Whittier was dead. That was also interesting. All around, she was an interesting girl. I took a puff and thought. Then I remembered the little item I had snagged by the pool.

The watch weighed in my hand like a tiny hand grenade. I hadn't seen one of these things in years, until Christmas Eve, when the little Bailey brat with the braids and the sniffles had been dangling one just like it. So now I had something in common with a kid named Zuzu. I laughed, but not for long. I turned the watch over. On its back, dead center, an ornate curlicue "G" was engraved. It was a shame, such elegant lettering, to reveal such a dirty secret.

G was for George, G was for guilty. George had been at the high school that night. He had also been inept, which was not hard to believe. I'd had my doubts about his Christmas Eve line, but this time there was no doubt. I snapped the watch case open. The crystal had been smashed and the watch stopped forever at twelve minutes past nine. The watch was as screwy as its owner. George couldn't even set his own watch straight. I stubbed out my cigarette. I was about due for another career, I figured, but not until I had it out with my one and only client the next morning.

The streets were quiet. Warm yellow light glowed from a few windows, and here and there strings of red and green bulbs outlined a few rooftops. Ribbons fluttered from the lampposts. Driving through Bedford Falls was like entering a Christmas card that had "Season's Greetings" signed in blood. I pulled up to the boarding house. Mrs. Parker had finished with her five-day foray into holiday cheer. She knew her limits. Her discarded Christmas tree was thrown out onto her curb. I saluted it, and dashed up the stairs into my room. Sleep hit me like a brick crashing to the floor.

The next morning Callaghan didn't even give me a hard time.

He was sitting at the side of the front desk himself, filling out some papers and whistling a happy little tune. He smiled at me with his ragged teeth. His eyes were as cold as ever. Despite the tune, jaunty he wasn't. But he was trying. He waved me towards the locked cell.

"Go on in," Callaghan said. "You can't get him in any worse a fix." Then he gave me a considering stare like he was trying to estimate my weight. He leaned his chair back against the wall and folded his arms across his chest. "Let's face it. Bailey didn't stand a chance with you as his gumshoe. Maybe it's time you both got wise to yourselves. Know what I mean?"

I didn't, but I said I had understood the words expressed.

"No, I mean it." He began his icy-eyed survey of me again. "You're a dopey guy working a dopey job for a dopey client."

"I get it. You think I'm a dope," I said. "It sunk in after a while."

Callaghan slowly leaned back to the desk top and picked up his coffee. "Take my advice, Incles. Get wise to yourself."

I started on my way towards the cell, then I stopped and faced him again. "Callaghan?"

He put down his pen. "Yes?"

"Has anyone ever told you that you have the most piercing blue eyes?"

I turned and whistled the rest of the way to the cell.

George was lying on his bunk with an open book over his face. I glanced at the cover, *The Mysterious Stranger*, by Mark Twain.

"George. Mr. Bailey," I said. I wanted to be angry but it was hard to be angry with a sap who gets hauled in for two murders in about as many days and falls asleep with a kid's book on top of his face. Callaghan was watching us from his desk. In the mid-distance, his whitish face hung like an empty speech balloon in a cartoon.

"Wha-huh?" George said. He jumped up as if yanked by wires, and the book fell to the floor. "Mr. Incles! I thought you might have given up on me. Glad to see you, stranger!" He poked his hand through the cell bars and shook my hand with enough enthusiasm to light up the Bedford Falls skyline.

"Keeping busy?" I said.

"Much as I can."

"You must have been pretty busy to land in here again. Guess you like the peace and quiet. Or maybe it's the food."

"Mr. Incles, you can't doubt me. Not now."

"I don't doubt you."

"I appreciate that, sir," he said in that earnest hicksville way he had.

"I positively disbelieve you."

"Mr. Incles, I - "

"You strike me as a nice guy. As nice a guy as ever offed two nasty pieces of work in a crummy little town.

You're the nicest killer I've ever met, and most of them, in my acquaintance, have been as nice as most other people, which is to say, not very. But you're a killer all the same. I tried not to think so. I tried to think maybe you were just a little nutty, a pleasant harmless kind of nutty like someone you'd meet in your dreams. Nutty as the name 'Clarence Odbody.' I tried to think that because, as I said, I like you. But I ran up against something harder than wishes and likes. Something in silver-plate and engraving."

He didn't flinch. Callaghan was still watching us, his blue eyes blazing cold like an unfriendly Siberian husky's.

I swung my right hand like a hypnotist. "I've got something of yours."

He followed my hand back and forth with his eyes a few times, and then he looked at me. "Mr. Incles?"

I pointed to my wrist watch. "I found it at the pool. Last night. The night Whittier was killed."

"Yes?"

I lowered my voice. "Cut the comedy, Mr. Bailey. I saw your little girl playing with the pocket watch on Christmas Eve. It even has your initial on its front."

"'G'" he said. Or maybe it was "Gee." He looked at me and rubbed his forehead. "I know this isn't my line of work, but it is my life on the line here, Mr. Incles. The only pocket watch I know about is the one Zuzu was playing with on Christmas Eve, and that one doesn't have my initial on it. It couldn't. That watch wasn't mine - Tom Partridge gave it to her."

It was a nice try. "But your wife or friends would have had it engraved for you, wouldn't they, George? Probably right away." I would have to check that out with the local jewelry shop. "Too bad for you they did."

George kept shaking his head. He wasn't a screwy guy with a screwy watch. He was a sharp operator. I'd entered the school about twenty-five minutes past eight, but the watch had stopped at twelve past nine. George had planted the watch with a fake time. He could place himself in a crowd scene that night. When the police found the watch like he wanted them to, and checked his alibi, they'd have to conclude that George was the victim of a frame-up, the most perfect alibi of all. He didn't know that I had ruined his little racket by finding the body sooner than he'd planned.

"Mr. Bailey, mind telling me where you were last night?"

"Well, sir, I was in the office and got home just after five o'clock. Mary and the kids and I had dinner. We had an apple pie, just the way I like it, with -"

"And then what did you do?"

"After dinner –"

"When would that be?"

"A little after six. The kids were finishing up the dishes and I was settling down in front of the radio, when my mother called. She's handy with the needle, and she'd been making a couple of dresses for the girls. She wanted us to bring the kids by so they could try them on. She'd invited a few neighbors over too. A regular sewing bee." He stopped and looked a bit sheepish.

Maybe he did have a remnant of shame. Already I could see the story shaping up: George Bailey in his ma's house, surrounded by a convenient truckload of rosy-cheeked alibis. They probably drank hot chocolate and had a sing-along. I bet George would be able to list the songs for me. It was so homey it made me sick.

"Fire away," I said.

"Well, the fact is, Mr. Incles, I didn't go."

"What did you do, Mr. Bailey?"

"I stayed home." He stood up and grasped the bars. "I was just tuckered out."

"You stayed home. Alone."

He nodded. "For a little while."

"A little while? From when to when exactly?"

He let go of the bars. "Not sure."

"You're not sure?"

"No. See, a little after Mary and the kids left, I went out myself. It was such a beautiful night - the sky, the stars, the moon." He pressed his face closer to the bars. His eyes glittered. "You know what I mean."

"No, I don't, Mr. Bailey. Why don't you tell me?"

"I went out to think about Clarence. Oh, I know, I know you don't want to hear about him." He raked his skinny white hand through his hair. "Neither does my wife. But when I walk by myself and talk to myself, I can almost feel like he's here again. It doesn't matter whether it's raining or snowing, I can feel him. Here." He tapped his heart. "And here." His fingers made fluttering motions all about him, like an interpretive dance of snow falling.

"You don't say." I reached for a pint of rye. Then I realized I didn't have one. "Mr. Bailey, is there anybody who can vouch for your whereabouts from, say, seven-thirty to ten o'clock on the night of Thursday, December 28th?"

"Only me," George said.

I think we both knew that as far as the police were concerned, that didn't mean much. But it did mean something as far as I was concerned. He probably didn't off Whittier. It was too risky to frame yourself and not set up a solid alibi. Somebody else must have planted the watch. I was still in business. It wasn't much of a business but it was better than nothing. George stuck his hand out again for me to shake. Our arms made like seesaws for a minute. I turned and walked out, past Callaghan. He gave me a milky blue glare. I went back to my car and thought.

If George hadn't planted the watch, I wondered who had. It was someone who had been at the gym. Someone who wanted to frame George. Someone who hated him, with a hate so strong it could only have begun as love. Someone who, when there was trouble, had still turned to George Bailey first. That one move told a lot. Blood ran as hot in Bedford Falls as it did anyplace else, and as cold, too.

CHAPTER TWENTY-SEVEN

The beauty shop door swung shut behind me and a tinkle of silvery-sounding bells announced my arrival. A heavy-set woman with a scalp full of shell-shaped pink clips sprouting all over her head sat in front of the mirror. Violet stood behind the woman, twisting the clips, and talking. The salon smelled of ammonia and floral perfume.

"Not too tight, is it, Mrs. Lambert?" Violet said. "Now, when this wave is finished, you won't know yourself!" She snapped in a last clip and frowned at me in the mirror. I leaned against the counter and watched.

"Be back in a jiff," she said. Her smile was sweet enough to spoon into black coffee. She came over to the counter. For me the sugar bowl was empty. "Yeah?" Her voice was like cold stones.

"We have to talk, Miss Bick."

"Not again."

"Right away. And alone."

"You see I got a customer. It'll have to wait."

"It can't. I could tell a story that would curl that gal's hair tighter than the permanent."

She looked at me, then the woman, then her wristwatch. "Seven and a half minutes," she said. "In the backroom. And that's it. Or the lady'll have hair she can scrub pots with. And don't let on who you are, Mr. Incles. She's a terrible gossip, and I won't have my business dragged into this."

The woman craned her neck towards us as far as she could. Her pink clips glittered in the light above the mirror. Her left eye focused straight at Violet. The woman looked like something rising out of the sea, but it wasn't Botticelli's Venus.

"What's going on?" she said. She had a high voice, out of breath and whiney like a tired child. It was disconcerting in view of her overall bulk. Then her eye fell on me. Her face broke into a fat-toothed grin as if she and I had been sharing secrets since before I was born. "And who's the fella?"

Violet flashed me a warning glance. I pursed my lips. I raised my left hand and let the wrist go limp as a week-old gardenia. I looked about the salon with diffident petulance. "Rosy colored light will give a warmer glow," I said. I stepped back to regard the wall. "Very flattering, to clients of a certain — maturity." The woman's grin became a glare. She pulled her neck back and stared at herself in the mirror.

Violet led the way into the back room. There was a single foldaway chair against the far wall, and Violet sat down in it. I leaned against the wall. She grinned and looked at me for more fun. But I was fresh out of it.

"Playtime is over, Miss Bick."

"What do you mean?"

"I think you've got pretty strong nerves, so I'll speak plainly. Why did you frame George Bailey for Whittier's murder?"

"Slow down, boy. What makes you think I killed Whittier?"

"Interesting. I didn't say you had, Miss Bick. Yet. But since we're here, together at last, why don't you tell me about you and George?"

"I don't get you."

"You're friends with George Bailey, Miss Bick?"

"Yeah. So?"

"So when did you realize George was much more than a friend? That he was the one you really cared about, the one you pretended all the others were, when the music went slow and the lights went down? The one you loved with a love so strange and spooky the only thing left for it to turn into was hate? Is that when you decided to do him in, and Whittier, at the same time?"

She looked at me and blinked. "Loved George Bailey with a spooky kind of love?"

The phrase had gotten to her.

She put back her head and laughed. In my life, I've known only three women who could do that and still look good. She was one of them. Her laughter didn't sound canned, either, but free and fresh, as if it was for real. "Mister," she said when her show of laughter subsided, "George just isn't that kind of fella."

"Are you that kind of gal?"

She raised an eyebrow. "For the right guy, I could be," she said. "Look, Incles, I admit once upon a time I was kind of sweet on George. When I was in high school." She lifted her chin and gave me a sidelong look. "Not that that was so very long ago. But long enough so I don't think of him as anything other than a friend. A good as gold, sweetest kind of friend."

That kind of talk always makes me itchy, especially when it comes from a blond with more length and curves than the Pacific Coast Highway, so I went on. "You were at the high school last night. Lose anything?"

"I wasn't at any high school. I told you."

"Anyone who can vouch for where you were?"

"I was at Martini's. I took a cab there. You can ask Ernie."

I would, but I could already guess what he would say. Anything to help out his sweetie. But he didn't know about her and Whittier. Maybe that would shake him up, and he'd spill.

"There's something else you can clear up, Miss Bick. Since the other party is unavailable. Just what is it Potter had on you?"

"I told you -"

"And I've told you, skip it. You have some racket going with this shop. Not a real receipt in the entire place. You didn't like it when I asked for one the other day. Pretty tricky if the tax man found out. Is that what Potter knew?"

She sat up straight.

"What did Potter want from you?"

She clenched her hands into fists and looked straight ahead at the wall. Then she turned to face me. "Let's say I tell you a little story."

"Sure."

"Let's suppose Potter wanted to ruin George Bailey. Completely, as a friend, and as a father and husband even. Let's say further that Potter wanted me to help him. To make people think George still had a thing about me. That we, you know," she gestured vaguely.

"I get it."

"I would refuse, naturally."

"Naturally."

"Say I had been making all my loan payments to Potter and he couldn't get to me that way. But suppose then he got hold of the account books for the salon and there were a few irregularities. Just the kind of thing to make a tax man sit up and take notice. Nothing that I didn't have a mind to make right this year. But let's say Potter said he would ruin me if I didn't help him ruin George. I'd have to figure I had no choice. I'd have to skip town. I'd need spare cash, quick, and I'd turn to George first, because he's the best friend a girl ever had."

"Just a friend, Miss Bick?"

"Wouldn't ask a question of me either."

"And in this fantasy of pure conjecture, would you tell

Whittier?"

"Charlie'd tell me not to worry, that he'd take care of it, that I wouldn't have to leave town. Let's say I wouldn't find out how he'd planned to take care of it until it was too late. He was my guy and I'd have trusted him. So I'd have changed my mind about ditching Bedford Falls."

"Because you didn't need to leave," I said. "Or wouldn't need to, if that's the tense we're still playing in. Because you knew Whittier took care of Potter. And that's how you know George Bailey didn't do it."

She looked at me steadily and said nothing.

"When Potter was offed, you got a measure of security. I wonder what you get a measure of from Whittier's death."

"Don't be a sap. I loved Charlie and if he was alive, I'd have gotten to spend all his money. I didn't have it in me to turn in him. I sure as shooting couldn't kill him."

It was a tricky little song she'd turned out. I wasn't too sure about some of the high notes though, and the lyrics needed a little work. One section she had dropped altogether: Whittier would have had it in him to turn her over if the heat ever came too close. "I don't suppose you would you be willing to sing this tune to the cops?"

"No, I wouldn't. I'm not planning on being done for accessory or anything else."

"I can just go to them myself."

"Without a shred of evidence."

"What about George?"

"They don't have much on him. They had to release him once already. Even without an alibi from me."

"Men have fried for a lot less."

"It'll never come to that. There's no sense in me getting in dutch over nothing. Get this straight, Incles. I never liked tattle-tales. And the police could make it look like I did Potter in, if they wanted to. Or at least that I was in on it."

"And as if you did in Whittier too," I said. "Or at least

that you were in on it."

She nodded her chin about a quarter of inch and kept looking at me. I did not blink.

"It never occurred to you, Miss Bick, that if the cops started nosing around, Whittier would have turned you in quicker than tumbleweed in a tornado."

"A girl in love doesn't think like that. Though I doubt you know about that kind of thing."

"I don't," I said. "He must have been quite a catch. Tell me, did he actually admit he killed Potter?"

"Not in so many words."

"In how many words then?"

"Alright, wise guy, none. But he kept saying Potter's death was a bigger bonanza than he'd ever hoped. And then he'd smile to himself."

"The will?"

"I guess so." She fingered the edge of her sleeve. "It sure was a lot of money."

"I wonder who gets it now."

"I don't know. Potter had some distant cousins over in Poughkeepsie I think. And Charlie's nephew is down in Delaware. Not me, if that's what you're fishing for." Violet looked at her watch and stood up.

I pushed myself away from the wall. "I've done enough fishing for one day."

I followed Violet back into the perfumed glare of the salon. The woman in the chair frowned at us.

"You're almost done," Violet said brightly. The woman stirred.

"If I'm not one-hundred per cent satisfied, I'm not paying a dime! I don't come here to get treated bad."

"Oh, him," Violet said. "Just a drummer pitching some hair oil. And you can bet I won't be buying from him, Mrs. Lambert."

"I know why," the woman said. Her face seized up as though she was about to sneeze. Her elbows flailed out in search of a couple of ribs to nudge. "He ain't got nothing to sell!" She embarked on a tinkling high-pitched laugh. It floated on the air and then it was gone.

It was a swell place and I liked being there. I liked playing a fairy for laughs and chatting with a good-time gal who curled hair during the day and did a few other things at night. She was a terrific gal. She was letting George Bailey sit in a cell for at least one murder she knew he didn't do. Maybe because, this second time, she needed someone to take the fall for her. Whittier had become a threat to her and she needed him bumped off. Maybe that night by the pool she hated him with a hate so strange and spooky that the only thing left for it to turn into was love. Women had done stranger things, although not recently to me.

I went to the door. Violet was unclipping the hair clips and chattering away. Bedford Falls baked some tough cookies. I went out.

CHAPTER TWENTY-EIGHT

Martini's was half-full. I stepped inside and looked around for the half that was empty. Uncle Billy was at the bar but I didn't feel like playing highway robbery today. I hunkered into the back booth. I figured I would see anyone coming my way. I figured wrong.

"Mr. Incles, how are you?" said a voice from behind me. I turned. It was Ernie Bishop. He was coming out of the back kitchen.

"I was hoping I'd run into you," I said. "I didn't know you'd gone into the cook business."

"Not cooking. Delivery. Martini was short of supplies and his van is in the shop. My shop, I mean. I'll be running orders here through the day, it looks like." He lowered his voice. "I've got a little horsemeat for you. Special."

"Have a seat. I'll buy you a drink." I had a few questions for him and I wanted him in the right mood.

"One's my limit. On duty, and in a hurry." Ernie winked.

I went to the bar and ordered two scotch on the rocks. The dark-browed bartender put the drinks in front of me and scowled.

"Nick, isn't it?" I said.

The scowl deepened and indicated its owner was named Nick.

"I thought you quit working here," I said. "Spread your wings and flew away to the bank. To work with Mr. Whittier, right?"

He scowled again. "You're a regular encyclopedia, stranger. I ought to buy you by the volume, and hang you on the shelf. Yeah, I did fly away. I got blown straight back." He stared glumly at me.

"A homicide'll do that."

He grabbed my collar and pulled me towards him. His right hand made a fist, which he put in front of my nose. He smelled of highballs, in a nice way. "What are you saying, mister? Say it if you've got something."

"You got this all wrong, Nick. I didn't mean anything. Honest." I raised a hand above the bar and made a boy scout salute. "Martini's sure lucky to get you back."

Nick pulled me an inch closer and breathed into my eyes. He gave me a little shove, and let me go. "Never got anywhere in this town. Never have, never will. Fly away? I've wished I could ever since I landed in this lemonade stand." He looked at me and cut himself short. He took a deep breath, put his right elbow on the bar, and extended his hand. It was either an invitation to arm wrestle or a demand for payment. I figured we had had a genteel sufficiency of each other's company. I gave him two dollars.

"Keep the change," I said.

He turned to the register and grunted.

When I got back to the booth, Ernie was tapping his fingers and grinning like a jack o'lantern that had survived Halloween night.

I put a drink in front of him and sat down.

"I was hoping I'd run into you, too," Ernie said. "I got to get a move on pretty quick, though. The boss likes the orders called in before two." He looked around and took a slip of white paper from his inside coat pocket. He folded the paper in half, put it on the table, and pushed it towards me. "Got it from Bert."

"So it'll be good."

"You can bet on it!" Ernie said. He jabbed his right index finger through the air with a flourish and laughed. He picked up his drink and downed it in one go.

This whole Potter business was making him as jittery as a junk addict. The hayseed joviality was an obvious cover. I wondered what Bert found out that I didn't. Maybe Potter didn't die the way we had all thought he had. Possibly the killer had poisoned him and used the money as a dodge, or the time of death was something you wouldn't expect. I'd seen that one a few times. I took the paper and opened it up. The handwriting was large and uneven, with heavy downward strokes.

"Miss Lily - Second.

Midnight Doll - Fifth.

Kerry May Sing - Ninth."

"This is what he's come up with?" I said. I was angry, but anger wouldn't get me far with Ernie. Bedford Falls was like any other town. It had people as treacherous as spiders, and as trusting as children. Except in Bedford Falls, most everybody fit into both categories.

Ernie was drumming his fingers faster than before and checking his watch. I lit a cigarette and looked at him. He had made a point of running into me and giving out information, but only the information he wanted to give out. Probably he knew I'd be onto him sooner or later, and he had planned this little get-together, complete with smokescreen and scam. He was a sly one. But not sly enough to know what I had on him from Potter's file. Maybe Ernie wasn't giving me the goods he thought I was after, but he was still telling me plenty.

"Yep. He's pretty good, ain't he, Bert?" Ernie said. "Helps to have friends in the right places." He winked again at me.

Ernie was a hardened gambler. I recognized the too-bright glint in his eyes, the restless tattoo of his fingertips, the eager optimism that was as chronic as cancer. So maybe Ernie's biggest problem wasn't the lure of a neon blonde, but the lure of fast horses and faster money. Ernie still had something to hide. Ernie bet big on dreams that hit the turf six, seven times a day, dreams with names like Kerry May Sing and Miss Lily, dreams that get printed up in small print at the bottom of the sports page and thrown away with the morning coffee grounds. The kids could go hungry and the wife grow haggard with worry, but still the dream must be fed. Ernie pinned his hopes on win, place or show, and he risked big. A habit like that would make it impossible for him to keep up on Potter's loan payments, and Ernie had been having trouble for about three months.

"How much you usually drop?" I said.

"Not much," he said. "Three or four."

Three or four hundred dollars, in a single afternoon. It was easy to see why Ernie was in trouble with Potter's bank, and it was worth knowing why, too.

"Put me down for two dollars, in the ninth," I said. I took out my wallet and slipped him two one-dollar bills. "But I'm not in your league, pal. Two dollars means two dollars. Eight quarters. Twenty dimes. Men in loud sports jackets and splashy wing-tipped shoes, men who smell of day-old alcohol and last week's promises, spend those same words at the trackside, day after day, only they're risking a hundred times more. No, I mean two dollars the way honest people mean it. People who try to make ends met by pinching a little here and there for themselves so their kids can have that train set they've been screaming about since Columbus Day. People you see every day on the sidewalks, waiting in laundry mats and at bus stops, and in offices, getting chewed out by the boss and taking it on the chin because they have to. And getting by as best they can. But you wouldn't see them here, not in a bar talking race tracks. You probably don't understand any of this, and I'm sorry for you. But I'll tell you something else. I'm even sorrier for your wife, and for your kids."

Ernie stared at me. His expression was difficult to read. "Okay, Mr. Incles." He looked a little white around the mouth. Reality hit him hard. "I'll see your order gets called in right away. You take care of yourself now." He slipped out of the booth and went for the door.

I'd had enough of setting the world right for one day. I paid my bill and left. I went into Gower's and bought a pint of rye. I went back to my car and took a swig. It was a long sweet swig and it felt pretty good. I thought about what I had to do next. I felt for the watch in my inside pocket. It was still there. Then I started driving.

CHAPTER TWENTY-NINE

A snowman was melting on the front lawn at 320 Sycamore, seeping imperceptibly but steadily into the dead brown grass around it. He was holding a shovel in front of him, with determined dignity, and he looked a little sad, as if he had been waiting there a long time while the upper half of him collapsed into the bottom. A black derby was centered on top, as upright as a hypocrite at a Sunday prayer meet. The sky had turned a noncommittal gray, with flashes now and then of cheerless yellow sunlight. I parked in front of the Bailey house and walked up the path. I knocked once, waited, and watched my breath.

The door opened a crack. All I could see was a side view of a pair of large, knuckled hands. I was about to speak when the door swung open completely. Mrs. Hatch took a long look at me, so I took a good look at her back, longer than I had before. Her dress was stylish, with a surprising flare to the skirt. Her shoes were a lot sharper than the ones her daughter wore. She was in her mid-sixties, with a short stiff wave of iron-colored hair that could stand up to anything nature threw at it, and prevail. Her face was powdered ear to ear with ivory talc. It looked as if it would crumble to dust if anybody touched it the wrong way.

Her eyes were brown, like her daughter's, but this woman's eyes had no hope. Eyes like that don't have any business on a face that's younger than the Egyptian pyramids, but the rest of her face had been working overtime to catch up. It was doing a pretty good job. Her lips twitched into a brief smile before they sank back to a preoccupied frown. Mary Bailey would probably look like this if she went on much longer fretting about George. Worse things happen in the world than a woman losing her looks to worry, but it would still be a shame.

"Please, come in," Mrs. Hatch said. "They've gone to see Mr. Bailey - Mary, and the children. Harry insisted on going too. But I expect them back any minute."

She led me into the living room and indicated an overstuffed chair. I took off my hat and sat down. She sat on the sofa, facing me. I noticed the Christmas tree was still going strong. A clock ticked thickly in the hallway. A car or two passed by on the road. We looked at each other with quick uneasy smiles, like patients in a dentist's waiting room.

"Have you found anything out?" she said.

"Things have looked worse."

"We never dreamed George would be in trouble this far along. It isn't a matter of finding out who killed those two men. It's just a matter of proving he didn't do it. Harry was saying that the other day. He says that you aren't up to - " she broke off. There was a pause. "I'm sorry, Mr. Incles."

"Harry says a lot of things. It must be easy to talk big. Maybe you get into the habit when you stand around on podiums a lot, picking up medals. I wouldn't know. Because I prefer to talk small, or medium, or not at all, and get things done."

"And just what have you got done, as you put it, Mr. Incles?" Her brown eyes held the merest flicker of a challenge. "No disrespect intended."

"What I have to say I'll say to Mrs. Bailey, my client. No disrespect intended."

"Of course. All I want is my son-in-law to come home. You can't imagine the torture it's been, to think of him in that - that place."

"I imagine that's why you're not there visiting him yourself."

She had cut-glass manners and it was hard to picture her as any part of the Bailey family. Or, as I could picture her saying, the Bailey family as any part of her. Somehow, even though she'd just been parroting him, I could imagine Harry Bailey putting that aquiline nose right of joint.

"I couldn't bear it," she said. "The trouble my men have borne. First my son, now my son-in-law. It's a terrible thing, Mr. Incles, for a mother to live to see her children pass."

She looked in front of her at nothing. Her eyelids drooped halfway. They were thin and white, like the eyelids of an elderly bird of prey. It must have been tough, watching Harry Bailey scoop up medals and glory while her own son was dead and buried. Harry Bailey was hard to take whatever way you looked at it.

There was a rattle at the door. It swung open and Mary Bailey swept in over the threshold. Her cheeks were flushed, and her scarf trailed halfway down her coat. A cold breeze filled the room. The four brats ran in after her.

"I beat you, I beat you," the little girl said. She whacked her brother on the shoulder.

Mary patted the girl's head and looked above it at me. Her eyes went serious but she kept her voice honey-coated. "There's some stale bread on the kitchen counter. Wouldn't you like to go out and feed that family of blue jays?"

"No," Zuzu said. "I just had a temperature."

The oldest boy looked at his mother. "Com'on," he said. He took the girl's hand. "It'll be fun." The brats trundled into the kitchen.

The front door was still open. Mary slipped off her coat and smoothed her hair.

She sat down in the chair across from me. She crossed her legs at the ankles. "You weren't waiting here long, I hope."

I was about to speak when Harry loped in. He swaggered, faintly weary with his own prowess, as if he were returning to the locker room after scoring the winning touchdown in the last minute of play. He would enter rooms like that into his eighties. He shut the door behind him and turned to face me. His hair was full of greasy kid stuff, and he was chewing gum. The negligent chomping stopped for a moment and he grinned.

"Sherlock!" he said. "Still pounding the sidewalk?" He didn't wait for an answer. "Won't need to much longer, I can tell you that much."

"No, I won't. As I was about to inform my client, here, Mrs. Bailey." I turned to her. "At least one-half of the case has come clean. Whittier did Potter."

"How do you figure that? The will?" Harry stood in the doorway, his hands on his hips, legs far apart, staking a claim to as much space as his cocksure frame would allow. "I wondered about that, too. Great minds, partner." He smiled. I didn't.

"I have some information the police don't have yet, Mrs. Bailey," I said. "My source won't talk to the police. Yet. For now, I'm following up on it, and I think there'll be enough to throw out the first count of murder. As for the second one, I have to confirm a few things, but I think I've got a pretty good idea. And I doubt the trail will lead to George."

Mary clapped her hands to her mouth. "I'm so glad we kept you on our side. George was just saying you were the best help we could have ever found. Why, he wouldn't stand for it today, when Harry told him you were just a - " She flushed. The Hatch women must have had tasty feet. They were always sticking them in their mouths.

"A what, Harry?" I said.

He came squarely at me, like a boxer in the ring. "A phoney-baloney shamus, and a no good coward to boot. Just what did you do during the war, buddy?"

"A 4-F," I said.

"Same as George," Mrs. Hatch said.

"Plenty of men who weren't at the front still helped win the war, Harry," Mary said.

"I'd have had to come home ice-cold in a body bag to gain your respect, Harry," I said. "With an arm blown off and a stomach full of lead."

Mrs. Hatch stood up. Her hands clenched spasmodically and her eyes were blank. She dashed out of the room, her heels clattering on the wooden floor.

"It'd be a start," Harry said.

"Harry, not again," Mary said. She stood up. "Thank you, Mr. Incles. I know George is in good hands. I'll tend to mother."

Harry had his arms folded up around himself tighter than a size three zoot suit on a size twenty gorilla. "Good work, Sherlock."

"Harry, I think it's time I let you in on a little secret, since you know so little and shoot off your mouth so much. If the police knew what I do, George would be one step away from the chair. I didn't see any need to upset Mrs. Bailey with this, but you strike me as the rock-solid type." I fished the watch out of my coat and swung it before him. "Ever seen this?"

He kept his eyes on me as he snatched up the watch. He flipped it over in his palm. He was turning pale around the mouth. He handed the watch back to me.

"No. Never." He started chewing his gum again.

"Take a good look. It won't bite."

"I've just told you all I know about it. Nothing."

"Recognize the initial? 'G'. Hmm. Could be Gregory, or Glenda, or Gary. Or how about George. Hey, isn't that the name of the police's sole suspect?"

"You're a regular laugh riot."

I slipped the watch back inside my pocket. "If the police saw this little item, we both know what they'd make of it. I can't say more, but I've got my own idea as to whose watch it is." Possibly Violet Bick had bought herself a watch at a pawnshop to smash on the gym floor and throw a little dust in our faces. And I liked saying something that would put soldier boy in a snit.

"Well, that's a relief," Harry sneered. "You've got an idea. Hope it doesn't die of loneliness."

"I'm howling," I said. "With frustration and ire."

Harry's chin moved from side to side. It was too sure of itself to be a quiver, but not sure enough to be a shake. He swaggered a step or two closer to me. "Let's just say I'm getting awful tired of seeing my brother in jail, mister."

"Don't sweat it."

"You oughta know a few things about yourself, pal," Harry said. "Before you think you can find them out about anybody else. Like why Mary hired you in the first place. George may say you've done a fine job, but he also says Clarence Odbody saved his life." Harry's eyes were trained on me, genial as an artillery piece. "Mary hired you with the express purpose of keeping an eye on you. She thought it was mighty fishy, the way you blew into town and suddenly there's a murder getting pinned on her husband."

I picked up my hat and stood up. "Mrs. Bailey is my client. It doesn't matter why she hired me so long as I get paid, and I'm allowed to do my job without interference. And maybe I would have put things together the same way she did, if I had been in her place. But that doesn't matter either. Mrs. Bailey should expect a result soon, Harry. I'd say in less than 48 hours."

"That's all we're giving you." Harry curled his upper lip, approximating a smile and exposing his two front teeth and the white wad of gum.

I went out the front door. The sky was lowering over the town like a steel lid over a garbage pail. On my way down the path, I stopped by the snowman and patted it on the head.

"Brother, let's hope we're on the right track."

I looked back at the house. Someone was watching me from the sitting room window. I waved. The curtain fell. I got in the car. It was time for another bite at Martini's.

CHAPTER THIRTY

The beefy bartender was scowling the same scowl as a few hours before. He gave me the same deeper-lined grimace for a greeting. Martini's looked the same. I went to the back booth and sat down. The same cabbie, with the same cap growing out of the side of his head like a mushroom, came out of the kitchen. He was whistling, but when he saw me he stopped short. His grin faded, and his short-legged, little dance-like skip stopped in the middle of a step.

"Hi, Mr. Incles. Everything okay?"

"Sure it is, Ernie. That is, it will be, once you sit down and have a word with me."

He hesitated. He lowered his brows, and jammed his fists into his coat pockets. His eyes tracked over to the half-empty bar, to the front entrance, and then back to me and the booth. Maybe he was planning his escape, or fishing for some free hooch. As far as I was concerned, it was no-go either way.

"Whatever you say," Ernie said. He slipped into the booth. He began drumming his fingernails.

"I got a question for you," I said.

"Shoot."

"Thursday night, the 28th it would have been, did you drop anybody off? I mean after dark, say, around eight o'clock."

He lightened up like a spring day after a heavy rain. "That's easy. Thursday nights around eight, I got a pretty regular customer. Violet Bick." He was cheerful and chipper as he spoke, as though he had no stake in Miss Bick's social engagements.

"Where'd you take her?"

"Over here. It's her hang-out, I'd guess you'd say." He picked up his fork and pointed to the corner table.

"Was she meeting someone?"

"Yeah. Some fella, guess she's hung up on. Must be to come here so often waiting for him."

"You don't know who she was waiting for."

"She never said." He shrugged. "Lucky guy though." He answered breezily, but maybe when I checked his story out with the charm school bruiser manning the bar, the breeze would run right out on him.

"Does Miss Bick call a cab at the end of the night?"

"Not as a rule. But this Thursday, she did. About quarter past nine. And she was madder than a wet hen. Looked to me like the guy didn't show. First time that ever happened, I guess." He grinned momentarily. "I took her straight home and she slammed the cab door shut so hard it almost busted." He shook his head and looked down at his drink. His face was serious and thoughtful. "A girl like that should never get stood up. It ain't natural." He looked up at me. "She's not in any trouble, is she?"

"No. Unless you know something I don't. I'm just earning my paycheck."

He glanced at his watch. "I better get a move on." He stood up and straightened his cap.

"So long, Ernie," I said. "I'll be in touch."

He smiled as enthusiastically as someone making an appointment for root canal work. I watched him leave by the front door. On his way out, he nodded at the bartender, who looked at him, raised his broken nose another inch, and went on polishing glasses. Ernie didn't even rate a scowl. I needed a drink. I went up the bar and took out my wallet. I rated plenty.

"You again?" Nick said. He stopped polishing the glasses.

"This time I'm on business."

"So am I, mister. The business is selling drinks. So how about you order one, or maybe two, and quit wasting my time."

"A scotch. Double. And one for you, Nick."

He put one glass in front of me and another in front of himself. "Don't go near the stuff much myself." Then his natural good nature reasserted itself. "That's another thing, bud. Where do you come off calling me Nick? I don't hardly know you from Adam's off ox."

"Let's do this Emily Post style," I said. "My name is Richard Incles." I put out my hand. Nick looked at it. He picked up his drink instead. "Mrs. Bailey's hired me to clear her husband."

"Yeah?"

"I'd like to ask you a few questions. Were you here Thursday night?"

"Yeah," Nick said. He took a swig. "Christmas week, I'm here every night, eight o'clock on. Some holiday, ain't it."

"Did you see Violet Bick here that night — that blonde number who runs the hair salon?"

"Sure, I saw her. She was here when I came on, and she stayed a while all on her own. It didn't look right." Half of his mouth attempted a smile.

"Maybe you thought of stepping in yourself?"

The other half of his mouth successfully wrestled the smile to the ground. His neck tensed up. "Hey, mister, I've had better looking dames stepping in on me. I don't trust frails, not with that color hair and that kind of walk. Not anymore." He looked into his drink.

I waited. "If you want to talk about it." He was already on his way.

"Velma. She was a singer. And she had some voice. One year she played Florian's, the Coconut Grove, and any other club you want to think of. We would have been married. But she got tired of waiting. She walked."

"A lot of soldier girls got tired of waiting for Johnny to come marching home."

He sneered. His mouth hardened and the blood in his temples seemed to thicken. "Velma was nobody's soldier girl, mister."

"Sorry, Nick. I didn't mean anything by it."

His scowl slumped into an expression of brooding self-pity. "She was easier on the eyes than any dame I've ever seen."

I got it. A down around the ankles kind of contralto that made you think of smoke and smooth scotch and silk stockings all at once. "I've got the picture. Long legs. Full mouth," I said. "A cool classy exterior that you wouldn't necessarily expect to see in a night club crooner, and a smile, when she really meant it, that lit up like the Fourth of July. Maybe her arm muscles were getting tired fighting off passes from the gentlemanly types who frequent gin and jazz joints. But maybe somewhere along the line, in the lonely hours of a rainy night, she met a fella who to the world was a swarthy tough and a heavy, but to her, he was just real sweet."

Nick looked me full in the face. He leaned forward and bared his teeth in a facsimile of a smile. "Mister, you want a knuckle sandwich?" His breath smelled of scotch. His glass was empty. "I know the tricks you peepers pull. Knowing things about me and I'm supposed to wonder how you knew them and get so nervous that I sing like two canaries and a steel guitar. Save your breath, bud. I've outrun and outbatted snoopers in every state of the U. S. of A." He shoved off from the bar.

"Look, Nick," I said. "I didn't come here to find out

about your love life."

"Sure. I know that." He gave me a steady look, not friendly, not unfriendly, as if he were considering the merits of a right hook versus a left one in relation to both sides of my nose. "So long, pal," he said. He picked up a cloth and began polishing the bar.

"You wouldn't remember anything else about Violet Bick that night?"

He went on wiping the bar. He didn't look at me. "She sat at the booth in back. She had one drink and took plenty of time with it."

"Remember what she ordered?"

"No, I don't. Want to make something of it?"

"That's good. It would have worried me if you had remembered. Know what I mean?"

He didn't look up.

"Anything else?" I said.

"She asked me to call her a cab."

"She seem worried, or nervous, or anything?"

"Let's just say I've seen happier faces."

"But not in the mirror," I said.

His upper lip curled like an angry mastiff's in appreciation of my witty remark. He moved to the far end of the bar.

I had sorrows of my own. Two witnesses placed Violet Bick at Martini's at the time Whittier was killed. That did in the second half of my theory. I took another swig. My glass was already empty. I was nothing for nothing. Almost. I had to use the only shot I had left.

CHAPTER THIRTY-ONE

"And hold the peppers this time. Last time you didn't. Right. For delivery, the police station." Callaghan hung up the phone.

"Rounding up the usual suspects, Callaghan," I said. "By process of elimination. Pepper, anchovy, maybe the red onion. Getting to the bottom of that case of indigestion."

Callaghan folded his lanky white hands in front of him. He said nothing and looked at me as if I were mosquito he had decided not to swot, out of curiosity rather than compassion.

I tried again. "Late to be ordering lunch."

"Some of us work for a living, Incles."

"So I've heard. But I refuse to believe such vicious rumors."

He gave a smile as sweet as a mouthful of cod-liver oil. "You've got business here, I presume."

"With you."

"What is it?"

"How about I told you a little story, Callaghan? About who didn't kill Potter, and who did?"

He grinned. He leaned his chair back to the wall and

put his hands up behind his head. On the desk in front him there was a pile of peanuts. "I like stories."

"This one I'll make real easy so you can understand it."

"Thanks. I always appreciate professional courtesy." He indicated a chair in front of the desk and scooped up a few peanuts. I sat down.

"What's your angle?" Callaghan said.

"It's like this. Let's say I have a source who tells me, positively, that George Bailey did not kill Potter. This source, for a variety if reasons, doesn't want to deal with the boys in blue, but if the need arises, this source is prepared to give George Bailey an alibi." I took out a pack of cigarettes and lit one. I flicked the dead match into the wastebasket and for once it went in.

Callaghan's eyebrows went up infinitesimally.

I went on. "Potter had a hold on this source, the way he did on most people in town. But what he didn't know is this source had a hold on Whittier. When Potter started bearing down too hard, Whittier stepped in."

Callaghan looked at a peanut a moment. Then he popped it into his mouth. "What kind of a hold on Whittier?"

"That doesn't matter here. What this individual didn't know yet was just how Whittier chose to intercede."

Callaghan shifted in his chair. "And how was that?"

"Whittier killed Potter."

Callaghan lurched forward. "No! Let me make a note of this." His blue eyes were like a pair of glass paperweights. "See if I've got all that you're saying. A source you can't name and who refuses to come forward says Bailey could not have done it. That should end the investigation right there. But wait. You have more. The source says that Whittier killed Potter. Any particular evidence on offer?"

"It all holds together, that's all. And that's a lot, actually, in my business."

Callaghan grinned. "And then Whittier conveniently

bashed himself over the head with a blunt object. Or maybe he decided he wanted a swim, so he dived into the water, looked down and realized he still had all his clothes on, and thumped himself in frustration at his own forgetfulness. That's a swell theory, too." He put a foot up on the table and nabbed another peanut. "You and me, kid, we can wrap this whole thing up in a jif."

I took a drag. I watched the cigarette butt blaze red and turn to ash. "I take it you're not convinced. Any particular reason?"

"Only a minor point. Just after eleven-thirty, Christmas Eve, Whittier was in here with me. Making a complaint. It seems he knew money was missing from the Building and Loan and he knew who had it: Potter."

"So?"

"Whittier and I went to make a friendly business call on the chump, to tell him the jig was up." Callaghan reached for another peanut. He gave me the full benefit of his eagle eye. "Whittier was with me when I discovered Potter's dead body."

"Maybe Whittier killed Potter just before he headed your way, right after I left. In which case calling you in would look good for Whittier, wouldn't it?"

Callaghan's smile opened up again, like a fistful of discarded scrimshaw. He was using up a lot of grins in one night. "No dice. I talked to Potter on the phone before we set out. Potter was alive when Whittier left, and he was dead by the time Whittier went back there, with me. So nuts to your theory." He picked up a peanut, and toasted me with it. "And to your source, if it even exists."

He gave me lingering look. "You know Incles, you're an even sadder case than I thought. I almost feel sorry for you. I bet you really thought you were onto something here. Let me tell you how it is. Bailey is guilty as Cain. Take my advice and clear out of town before you get laughed out." He picked up a handful of peanuts and downed them in one go.

"I thought I was supposed to get wise to myself," I said. "Can I do that if I get out, or do I need to get wise first? Or can the process be simultaneous? Do you mind getting hit with questions faster than you can answer them?"

Callaghan stopped in mid-peanut. His jaws gave one last grind. "Dust," he said. He picked up a pen and turned back to his paper work.

I headed out. It had already been a long day. I sat in the car and lit another cigarette. I thought about what it would be like to have a long smooth swig of rye. I could already taste it. I daydreamed about a couple of criminals, both bad and one beautiful. I had a glimpse of blond hair, a woman with long legs and a tall white-faced man beside her. They met and parted as smooth as shadows on still water.

Maybe Violet and George were in this together. I saw myself chasing them down a dark and lonely road, over a bridge, in a heavy snowfall. A fat lady suddenly appeared and got in my way. She had her hair in pink curlers and she was laughing as if she was seeing herself in a fun-house mirror. I struggled past her through the snow.

Maybe Violet and George had exchanged murders. Maybe Violet did Potter for George, and George did Whittier for Violet. Maybe they were sure the cops would believe Whittier did Potter, or that some sap like me would try to make the cops see it that way. But Whittier turned out to have an alibi. So maybe once George was strung up for both, Violet saw her chance to double-cross him too.

Or maybe dreaming about hooch was worse than drinking it. I was generating maybes like gerbils and getting nowhere. I started the car, and headed over for a pint of inspiration.

CHAPTER THIRTY-TWO

I drove towards the center of town, and turned onto Franklin. A gray sedan pulled out of one of the side streets. It stayed with me a block or two. I slowed down to allow it to catch up with me, but it declined the opportunity. After another block, it turned right, into a side street. I drove on and pulled up across the street from Gower's. The sky was dark and cold. It looked like snow.

Gower and a freckle-faced kid with a baseball cap were behind the counter. A step-ladder stood beside them. The kid was restocking the candy shelf. He had sleepy eyes that blinked in the light as if he had spent all day in the picture show. He unscrewed the top of a big glass storage bottle and replenished Gower's supply of cinnamon hots. He looked up when I came in and moved to wait on me.

"That's okay, son," Gower said. "I'll get it." He turned to me. "Anything I can get you?"

"A pint of rye, please."

Gower turned and reached up to the shelf for it. He put it down on the counter. "That all?"

"For now. I'll come by for the hangover pills later. First things first."

Gower smiled as crisply as a pressed shirt. It was a brief

and polite smile that never got rumpled and could be put straight back in the box after use. It was the smile of someone who wanted to get back to what its bearer had been doing, and who may have had something to hide.

"While you've got that ladder out, Ned," Gower said, "you may as well make sure that clock is wound." He looked at me. He studied my face a minute as though I might need winding up, too. He rang up my purchase. I pocketed my change. He had given me an idea.

"You wouldn't happen to know what time it is, Mr. Gower?"

He looked pointedly at the large clock above the cigar display. "Twenty past four," he said.

"Is that right? I'm pretty sure it's running slow."

He pressed his lips together. "If you would like, I'll check it against my own timepiece," he said. He pulled out a pocket watch. He snapped it open and looked at it. "Twenty past four. Plus four seconds."

"Thanks. You know, I haven't seen a watch like that in quite a while," I said. "With a second hand and all."

"It was my daddy's, and my granddaddy's, and his daddy's before that." He held it out to me. "Have a look, young man."

It was surprisingly heavy, like the weight of a dead body. The case was antique silver. On the back, in ornate lettering, was engraved: Gower. The lettering had collected too much tarnish to be a recent addition. Gower had been most accommodating this afternoon. I turned the watch over in my palm, and handed it back.

"Thanks, Mr. Gower."

"Not at all."

I picked up my bottle. "I bet you're real careful of that watch."

"Indeed I am." He stood behind the counter, his back straight and his hands resting palms down the counter.

"You wouldn't let it get near water, or smashed in a scuffle, or anything."

"Surely not."

The kid kept rattling shovelfuls of candy into glass bottles. I turned and left. Gower stood and watched me.

A wet heavy snow was falling. I went back to my car. A woman hurried by, carrying a bag of groceries. A red-haired brat of about four trundled behind her. The kid was tossing a ball in the air. The ball hit the ground and rolled away from him into a doorway. The brat careened after it. A man in a wide-brimmed hat was standing in the doorway. At the boy's approach, the man drew back sharply. He opened a newspaper and held it wide in front of his face. I sat in the car and had a swig. It felt good. The second swig was even better. The man in the hat was still eye-deep in newsprint when I pulled out.

CHAPTER THIRTY-THREE

I drove by a gray sedan that was parked in front of Violet's shop. No crime in that. The city was probably full of gray sedans. All the same, I slowed down. Shops and offices were letting out for the day. It was a cold night. Men kept their faces as far down as they could into the neck of their coats. Women's high heels tripped quickly along the frozen pavement. A bus rattled noisily down the road.

I stopped at a set of red lights. A broad-shouldered man, with a wide-brimmed hat, was lumbering down the sidewalk as amiably as a Sherman tank. People walking in pairs separated to let him through, no questions asked. He passed by a shop front. The white light glared an instant on his face. It was Nick. He had a newspaper folded under his arm. No crime in that, either. Necessarily. The lights changed. The car up front had trouble starting and the white Plymouth ahead of me started honking like a Canada goose stranded in the middle of a pillow factory. Nick looked up. He saw me. He turned down a side street. The turn was a shade abrupt for my liking, but he hadn't asked me.

I drove on to Mrs. Parker's.

Mrs. Parker had fallen asleep in the front room. A duster trailed from her left hand. Several afghans lay across her knees. I slammed the front door and woke her.

"Sakes alive!" she yelped. She regained composure. "You're back." She clutched the uppermost afghan tighter. She did not appear pleased.

"I'd have to wake up pretty early in the day to get anything over you, Mrs. Parker." I unbuttoned my overcoat.

"Don't get smart, young man."

"Don't worry. I've tried. It's too much work."

Wisecracking had as much effect on her as a horsefly would on the progress of the Queen Mary.

"You got something in the mail this afternoon. Special Delivery." She reached into her afghans and drew out an oversized envelope. She weighed it in her hand and shook it a bit. "Not your birthday?"

"No, ma'am."

She held the envelope out to me. "I don't wonder that somewhere some gal must be pining after you."

"Not that I know of."

"Even if it is just your mother."

"Thanks, Mrs. Parker." I took the envelope. It was postmarked Albany, and it had a nice heft to it.

"I take it you've been pretty busy. Hear tell you may have things wrapped up in a couple of days," she said. "Not that it's any of my business. But I'll need to know if you're leaving so I can rent out that room."

"I'll let you know."

"Yep, I hear all kinds of things." She wound the end of the duster around her finger. I headed up the stairs.

"Mind, I never would have guessed all the folks around here that get themselves into financial trouble. No siree. Myself, I just take a small loan, for general upkeep." Her voice followed me. It passed me on the stairs and turned around to face me. "Not like some people in this town. Buying up cars and hair salons left, right and center, and then falling behind in the payments. Of course, it isn't my fault if the clerk left early one afternoon and my last payment got marked late. I can't mind everybody's business for them."

My room had the fake lemony smell of Mrs. Parker's furniture polish. The bed was made. A fresh towel had been put out. Mrs. Parker had been straightening up. The manila file was laid out by the phone, for my convenience. I sat down on my bed and opened the envelope.

There were a few pages of handwritten notes, an obit, and a grainy wire service photo of Morrisey. It was the one I had already seen, except this one was shot with a wider angle and had a few insets pasted in around Morrisey's face. An overexposure of an assembly line tough was inset on the left. It was captioned "Clement Walters." You could see he had two eyes and a mouth. He was looking at you straight on but something about him looked like he was giving you his profile at the same time. It as if he was so used to having mug shots taken that he gave all angles to the camera at once. Above the tough-nut, there was a picture of a pale young man in a police uniform, captioned "William Anders." He was one cookie that could have used a few more minutes in the oven. To the other side of Morrisey, a shot of a jail was pasted in.

I poured myself a drink and turned to the obit. Morrisey had died in July, 1945, two months after his release from a three-year jail sentence on corruption charges. He had drowned off Crane's Beach in what the obit called "questionable circumstances." Probably Morrisey had offed himself. His career had first come to scrutiny in the early forties, after the escape of a key state witness. Then there turned out to be a lot more worth scrutinizing. William Anders, a youngster with two years in the department, had blown the whistle on Morrisey. The papers must have loved that angle. I didn't, particularly. I took a swig. So what, I thought. So a cop gets greedy and goes rotten. I didn't see why Potter would care.

The notes had a little more meat to them but not much. Morrisey had started out in New York. He was ambitious, and within his first three years, helped bust two bank robbery rings in the northern New York state. That's how it looked, anyway, when it happened, during the late twenties. Afterwards, at his trial, it turned out one of those rings had offered Morrisey his first bribe, and he accepted. The brains behind the operation were never so much as booked. I leaned my back against the wall. This stuff at least tied him to the right state, and maybe it was his link to Potter.

But it still didn't explain why Potter would hold onto that newspaper story for four years. I reached for the file and looked at the clipping. Little Morrisey was still frowning and in trouble, Clement Walters was still on the run, and nothing still made any sense.

I put the little photo alongside the new one. I looked at the wide-angled photo, and then at the first one. There was something vaguely familiar about the second photo. Looking at it and trying to get at what there was about it was like trying to hum a tune you couldn't quite recall. So then you just made yourself decide the tune didn't exist, that maybe you had dreamt it, just so you could get on with things. But it still nagged. One day, maybe when you weren't chasing it anymore, it comes to you, blaring out from a radio in the doctor's waiting room. Until then, you kept going. I tapped my finger over Morrisey's face. It was weary and had sad, humorous eyes.

"Hi, Morrisey," I said. "I know the feeling."

It didn't make any sense. I poured a drink, and took another look at the loan applications. I had checked into two of the dossier's four applicants, Violet and Ernie. I had kept my eye on them pretty well. So far, I had come up with answers, but not to the questions I had in mind.

That left Mrs. Parker and Tom Partridge. Mrs. Parker was only one month behind on her payments, and it was hard to see her killing Potter or Whittier over that. It was hard to picture her keeping her mouth shut afterwards, too. So that left Tom Partridge. All I knew about him was that he was the principal of the high school, that he was in debt to Potter, and that he had given his watch to Bailey's brat in front of a crowd. It was a pretty fancy thing for a man in debt to give away. I looked at his application. His address was 125 Monroe, a few lots down from the high school. I smoked a cigarette. It was time to have a chat.

I slipped the file inside my coat and headed down the stairs. Mrs. Parker wasn't in the front room. I opened the door.

"Don't slam that door," she called out. It sounded like she was in the kitchen.

I got in the car and headed over to Partridge's. The snow had turned to frozen rain. The roof of my car was leaking. I was getting cold. I took a small swig to keep me warm, then another one to keep me happy. The third one was to celebrate the joy of living.

I drove a few blocks. A car pulled out behind me from a side street. It tried to keep its distance, but the rain made it nervous and it nosed up too close. It was the now familiar gray sedan.

I sped up, drove a block further, and then wheeled around sharply. My brakes squealed on the wet pavement. I caught a glimpse of the sedan turning right onto Franklin. The driver wore a hat low over his face. He also had his foot to the floor. The car was a block and a half away when I got to Franklin. The rain battered the windshield. I started the wipers but the street still looked blurry. I had the sedan in view to Main Street and across it and all the way to Monroe. The car headed down Monroe, just beyond the high school, and turned left into a side street, proceeding at speed, and took a sharp right. I followed, but by the time I made the right, the street was empty.

I drove back to Monroe and pulled over. The rain beat down steadily. The street was dark and quiet. It was lined with modest houses, each one with a front lawn the size of a large sand box. These were the houses that had made George Bailey so beloved in this burg. I got out of the car and found number 125. The house was dark, except for the light over the front door. I knocked. No one answered. I went around back. A red De Soto was parked there. The engine was cold. Talking with Partridge would have to wait. But by now I had decided there was another friend I wanted a chat with, over a drink and with a clenched fist.

CHAPTER THIRTY-FOUR

The dinnertime crowd was starting to drift into Martini's. Low laughter rose from a few tables in back. A burly sourpuss of a man sat alone at the bar, staring into the drink in front of him. His hands rested in front of him like a pair of weapons waiting to be taken up and put to heavy use. At the other end of the bar, Nick was polishing glasses. His eyes were baleful. I went up to the bar. Nick went on wiping the glasses. Then he pushed off in my direction. He went past me and stopped in front of the sourpuss.

"Mr. Walsh, you done?" Nick said.

"Naw. I'm okay," the sourpuss said.

Nick glanced in my direction, scowled, and turned back to the man. He put his elbows on the counter and rested his weight on them. "Martini's due back any minute now," he said. He pumped his voice up a few decibels. It was as hard and unyielding as a flexed bicep. "He told you not to come back in here, ever. Now, myself, I don't mind. A scrape's a scrape. But that Bailey guy you slugged is Martini's best friend. So how's about you clear off." Nick folded up the terrycloth towel, snapped the air with it, and slung it over his shoulder. He swaggered over to me.

"Looks like the place is crawling with friends of George Bailey," Nick said.

Walsh hovered over his drink, swallowed the last of it in one go, and shuffled out of the bar.

"There's someone you should talk to," Nick said. "That geezer gave Bailey a sock to the jaw. Saw it myself. Christmas Eve."

"Actually, Nick, you're the one I'd like to talk to."

"Yeah?"

"But then I say that to all the two-bit thugs who wear an oversized hat and follow me around in a gray sedan."

His mouth dropped open a couple of inches. "Huh?"

"And another thing. That open newspaper trick. It stinks."

"Mister, you need a drink worse than I thought."

"I wouldn't want to overwork you. In fact, I'll make it easy for you." I pushed my hat back on my head. "I'll be here an hour so. I'll be taking the back booth there and I'll order dinner, probably the steak. Medium rare. Then I intend to gobble a martini or two. When I'm done with that, I'll look up Tom Partridge. I was out his way this afternoon, but you already know that. I'll talk with him for as long as it's interesting. Then I expect to head back to my room at Mrs. Parker's. I sleep eight hours, when I can. I like my coffee with cream, no sugar. You got that? Or you want to write it down?"

"Brother, you don't know what you're playing with. There's nothing I don't remember and nothing I don't get even with."

"I'll take my chances. Along with Velma."

Nick leaned closer to me and made a fist. Since it was so in fashion around here, I made a couple of fists myself.

"Nick, you make trouble again?" Martini said. He was standing by the entrance. He still had his hat and coat on. He shook his head and came towards us. "Sit down, my friend. Nick, the glasses not finished."

Nick glowered. He went back to work.

I sat in the back booth and had the special, medium rare, and a martini, then another. Nick didn't look in my direction, even when I got up and went out the door.

I headed over to Tom Partridge's. There wasn't a gray sedan in sight. A light was on in the front window. I went up the front door and knocked. Tom Partridge answered. He was smoking a pipe, breathing calm and mortgaged resolve while he took up the width of the doorway.

"Yes?" he said.

"Mr. Partridge, my name is Richard Incles. You may remember we met at Martini's a few days ago. I'm working for Mrs. Bailey, to clear her husband. I'd like to ask you a few questions, if that's okay."

"Young man, I'll do anything I can to help George Bailey," Partridge said. I'd heard that one before.

Partridge stepped aside and ushered me in. It was a small house, dark and heavy with too much mahogany furniture. A large oval dining table was wedged into the space beneath the bow window. There wasn't enough room for the end chairs, and they were crammed against each other in the corner of the room, collecting dust. It was a dining table that belonged in a house with a billiard room and a snooty butler. The Partridge's front room smelled of pipe smoke, carpet dust, and grilled pork chops.

I was sniffing the air and trying to remember the charms of home when a small, sad-eyed woman came into the room. Her legs were as skinny as toothpicks, and her heels were too high and too heavy for her. She dragged them after her like ice skates. She wore round wire-framed glasses and carried a book. She smiled wearily, out of duty. Her husband took charge of saying the hellos around here. She had entered the room like a good-bye, just hanging in the air, waiting to get said.

"Sarah, I was going to fetch you," Mr. Partridge said. "This young man is Mr. Incles. He's helping George Bailey. He'd like to ask us a few questions."

She melted silently into the nearest chair. I bet she had

done a lot of silent melting in her time. She smiled briefly again, and winced as if the effort of sitting or smiling or both pained her.

"Sit down," Mr. Partridge said. I sat but did not melt. Mr. Partridge took an overstuffed brown chair across from me. The chair surrounded him with a new layer of bulk that accrued to him like good fortune. "Now what can we do for you?"

"As part of my investigation, I've been going through the names of those who owed money to Mr. Potter, to eliminate them as suspects. I'm sure you understand."

He looked at his wife. Mrs. Partridge nodded. "Indeed I do," Mr. Partridge said. "Go right ahead."

"I take it you owed a fairly substantial amount to Mr. Potter. Is that right?"

Mr. Partridge looked at his wife again. This time she did not nod. "Yes," Mr. Partridge said.

"I also take it that you fell behind in your payments. Correct?"

"You certainly do your homework, young man." Mr. Partridge smiled easily and blew some pipe smoke into my face. His wife coughed delicately into the palm of her hand.

"I was two, three months behind," he boomed.

"Was Mr. Potter putting any pressure on you, Mr. Partridge?"

"He was. Him and his poker-faced goon both. I got a couple of nasty letters from them right before Christmas." He took another puff. "I didn't let it get to me."

"Why not?"

"I knew something had to give. My luck was due to change. I'm a great believer in luck, Mr. Incles."

"You even gave your family watch away, on Christmas Eve. To one of the Bailey children. Wasn't that a bit extravagant?"

"Not at all. I bought that watch at a rummage sale, a few years ago, to time races for the high school track meet.

Cost me all of a dollar. But kids don't know the difference."

"And the debt to Mr. Potter?"

"Paid it all off yesterday. Every cent."

"How's that, Mr. Partridge? Did your ship come in?"

"More like my horse." He winked.

His wife coughed long and loud. She waved a hand at her husband. "Tom, please. A glass of water." Her voice was worn thin with coughing.

He stood up and hurried out of the room.

"Thanks for your time, Mrs. Partridge."

She nodded.

I ran my finger along the coffee table beside me. It had a scalloped edge and a carved inset of lighter wood on its legs. "Beautiful furniture."

"It was the pride of Beacon Hill," Mrs. Partridge said.

"You had this shipped all the way from Boston?"

"Yes, that's where I'm from, originally. And where we met, Tom and I. Tom was invited to be headmaster of Groton, a fine boarding school out that way. Perhaps you've heard of it. But that was years ago. Yes indeed." She fingered the edges of her book. "My husband had his pick then. He could have gone places."

"Bedford Falls is a place," I said.

"Bedford Falls is home," she said, in a tone that closed the discussion as surely as a bank vault. She looked me flat in the eye. Her eyes were still a defiant baby blue.

Mr. Partridge came back spilling a tumbler of water. I stood up.

"That all, young man? No long grilling under a bare light bulb about my whereabouts? I'm disappointed."

"You read too many detective novels, Mr. Partridge."

He looked at my feet. "Is it true you folks wear gum-soled shoes or is that a joke?"

"It's no joke," I said. "They double as an eraser when I make too many mistakes."

He grinned. Mrs. Partridge remained seated, smiled,

and said goodbye. I was right. This was when she came into her own. I thanked them again for their help, walked out to my car, and drove to the boarding house.

I had something to think about. Partridge at least had ties to Boston, and that maybe meant ties to Morrisey and the press clipping. It was the closest connection I had so far.

I parked across from Mrs. Parker's, under a streetlight. Something was still nagging me. I pulled the file out of my coat and looked at the two photos again. I held the larger one up to the light. I turned it around. I was looking at that mug who gave you his profile even while he was looking at you straight on. I looked at him closely. I brought the photo up to my face, and laughed.

I had been seeing him every day for the past week. Clement Walters was Nick the bartender.

I pushed my hat back on my head. I pounded my fist on the steering wheel. I felt like I had just downed a few measures of the kind of hooch you only dream about. "Steady, fella," I said. Then I got out of the car. I was standing beside the trunk of the car fishing around for my room keys. The hedge of hydrangea bushes in back of me was tall and dark. Anybody waiting for me would have had a wide open shot at the back of my head.

Somebody took it.

CHAPTER THIRTY-FIVE

"Jesus, Mary and Joseph," a voice above me said. I opened my eyes. Someone shot a beam of white light into them. It felt like a dentist's drill going into a nerve. I winced, shielded my eyes with my hand, and tried to sit up. I couldn't. I rolled my head back and looked up at a cold, three-quarter moon. Mist rose over me. Maybe this was heaven. Mrs. Parker's face swam out at me. Maybe it wasn't.

I raised my head as high as I could, about half an inch or so, and took a gander. I was on the sidewalk in front of her boarding house. I'd seen better sidewalks, though not often this close up. Mrs. Parker had a man's overcoat thrown over her afghan. She tugged at her collar and her chin quivered. She peered at me more closely. From the point of her chin to the beginning of her hairline she was smeared with greasy face stuff. It gleamed greenish-white in the dark.

"What sort of trouble are you running with, Mr. Incles?"

"I'm okay, thanks," I said.

"Don't get smart, young man. I am a landlady, not an emergency unit. Though you wouldn't know it from what I have to do around here."

My hat was still on. I pushed it up and rubbed the back of my head. I had a bruise the size of Nebraska. "You didn't happen to see anything, did you?"

"No, I did not. You're supposed to be the private eye, aren't you?" She sneezed. "If I don't catch my death out on this sidewalk, I don't know. I was in the middle of my facial regimen. I heard a thud outside and then some footsteps running. About four minutes ago." She glanced at her wristwatch. "Yes. One man's footsteps, I'd guess. Which way he was going, I don't know." Her hand disappeared into the many folds of cloth surrounding her and emerged clutching a handkerchief. She sneezed again and wiped her nose accusingly. Then she crossed her arms tightly as if to keep herself bound together. "They take anything off you?" she said sharply.

I felt for the file. It was still there, bent double against my stomach. So was my wallet, and my gun. Nobody wanted to kill me. Not this time. "Not a chance," I said. I rubbed the back of my head again. Now I had a bruise the size of Texas. I could guess whose calling card this shiner was, and what kind of visit he'd plan on paying next time.

"I will have to call the police about this, you realize," Mrs. Parker said. Even out on the front steps, Mrs. Parker had a nasal whine tailor-made for cutting into a twelve-party line. "That nice Mr. Callaghan. A real solid policeman. I doubt he's ever gotten himself into a fix like this. He'll get to the bottom of it alright."

I stood up slowly. My legs hurt. At least that meant they were still there. I leaned against the hood of my car and steadied myself. I turned around slow and easy like a chicken on a rotisserie, until I was facing her. "You run a respectable establishment, Mrs. Parker. You don't want reporters crawling all over the place, asking questions and turning things up, and then turning those same things upside down, for everyone to read about over their cornflakes."

She sniffed and tightened her collar. Her mouth pursed up. It was small and dark and looked like a prune dropped into a plate of light green cream. "I see what you mean."

"Let it be our little secret, Mrs. Parker."

She thought it over. Then something occurred to her. "You will let me know any developments straight away, I expect."

I nodded.

"You better come inside and get yourself fixed up. I can't do with a tenant sprawling out all night on my sidewalk. It's bad for business."

I squared my shoulders. Pain shot through them from right to left and back again. I straightened my hat. "Sorry you were put to so much trouble, Mrs. Parker," I said. "You go in and finish that regimen. There's something I have to get done tonight. But I'll be sure to be real quiet when I let myself back in."

She looked at me a moment. Her dark brows jerked a bit like twin minnows in a saltwater net.

"Suit yourself," she said. She walked up the front path. Her greenish face floated in the dark in front of her. She entered the house, and shut the door. The lock gave a decisive click.

CHAPTER THIRTY-SIX

I scanned the joint as I entered. It looked the same as it had the other times I had been there today, except now Martini was behind the bar. I headed over to him.

"Hello, boss," I said.

"Mr. Incles, you are getting to be a regular. You like the food here, eh?"

"It's either that, or the company." I leaned onto the bar and drummed my fingernails. I looked towards the kitchen in back. No one was in view. "Speaking of which, where's Nick?"

"Nick? Tonight, he never showed. I have such trouble with that one." He shook his head. "But he's not a bad soul."

I tapped the left side of my chest. "A heart of gold."

"Hey Mr. Martini," a voice to the right of my shoulder said, "you going to talk all night, or get us some drinks?" I turned and confronted some frenzied pink plumage. Underneath it was Violet Bick.

Mr. Martini smiled. "I'm getting to it, my lady."

"A scotch for me," I said.

"Make that two," Violet said.

So Lover Boy had sent her over here to find out how

151

much I knew, in case I came by looking for him, which I imagine he expected I would.

"You're pretty sure of yourself, Miss Bick," I said. "I imagine you could make a man forget anything." I took out a cigarette and lit up. I leaned my right elbow on the bar and regarded her through the haze of smoke. "Even a songster named Velma."

Her eyebrows tensed. "Who's that?"

"Don't tell me you're so good you can make yourself forget, too."

"You're a kick, mister, but not when you talk in riddles."

"So I'll try telling you a story instead. With pictures too, and this one doesn't have a hypothetical thing about it. I think you'll want to be sitting down by the time I've finished. I take it you're by yourself."

"Not anymore." She grinned. Pretty women in a joint like Martini's, they can't resist flirting, especially when it's with danger. "I'll get us a table." She walked off with a full set of curves nobody could ever improve upon.

Martini set two drinks down in front of me. I paid him and found Violet. I sat down and looked at her.

"What I love about this set-up is how everything runs to type," I said. "The ex-con with the broken nose and the bench-pressed scowl. The hooch joint singer who did a runner and left a hole in his big dumb heart as wide as a cannonball. The town sweetie who's as good at fixing hearts as breaking them when she wants to be, and I bet you can be a lot of things when you want to be. The grim-faced banker without a soul who turns to blackmail and gets too greedy, and his granite-eyed goon who's even worse. And the town that seems decent and simple, until you look closer. Then you see how long the shadows fall. You hear the howls of despair and frustrated ambition, and you catch the smell of fear."

She took a small neat sip and looked at me. "Don't forget the paperback gumshoe with last year's lapels and a tough guy patter that went out with Herbert Hoover."

"All the same, you're willing to talk to me, or at least listen. You want to know what I've found out. So I'll tell you. And when I've finished, I bet you'll be willing to sing to the police like a canary and a three-stringed banjo."

Her face gave no expression.

I took out the envelope sent from Albany. Then I took out the picture of Clement Walters. I laid it flat on the table in front of her. "See that face?"

"Yeah."

"Remind you of anyone?"

"No."

"You're not trying. Look again."

"All I see is a nose, two eyes and a mouth. A lot of people meet that description. If they're lucky."

"It's Nick," I said.

She shrugged and looked at it more closely. "So maybe it is. How about that." She took another sip, this time more of a swig. She was getting impatient. "Who cares?"

"I think you do, Miss Bick, very much. Four years ago, Nick operated a bad checks ring out of Boston. Only then his name was Clement Walters. He was in the can, due to turn state's evidence. Then he escaped, came here, and began a new life. Or tried to."

"What does that have to do with me?"

"Potter found out who Nick was. He started to blackmail Nick, and Nick had to kill him. But Whittier also knew about Nick's past. Nick went to work for Whittier because it was the perfect inside track for a fraudster. Only Whittier started putting the squeeze on him too. Maybe Whittier figured out that Nick had bumped off Potter, and had more to hide than ever. So Nick had no choice. He put an even bigger squeeze on Whittier. Nick's scared of what I know. He came by today and left me a little a something. Nothing I can't handle. And in case I came by looking for him, he left you here to wait for me." I took a swig. "Again, nothing I can't handle."

She lifted an eyebrow. "Mister, you'd be surprised."

I went on. "When you see Lover Boy, you can tell him everything I told you. He already knows I don't scare easy."

"Huh?" she said. Her top feathers wavered, then stood still. "I've listened but you don't make a lot of sense, Incles. Try again."

"Alright, I'll spell it out for you slowly, Miss Bick. And then you'll spell it for the police even slower. Callaghan will appreciate that. You and Nick are lovers. You're in this together. Potter tried to blackmail Nick, so Nick killed him. But that didn't end it. Not by a long shot. Whittier stepped into Potter's shoes, and he was as greedy as his boss, maybe more. So you got friendly with Whittier. It was good for business. Nick understood that. Whittier never knew about you and Nick. You and Nick made sure no one knew."

"Mister, you've got me mixed up with every man in town. I'm not that bad."

"Miss Bick, I'm willing to bet you're that good."

She blushed, but I was only getting started.

"All along, it's been you and Nick. He's the brawn and you're the brains. The bad and the beautiful. You buddied up to Whittier just so you could get close enough to kill him. I saw you with him by the pool that night. You were laughing then. But you're not laughing now."

Her eyes were fixed on me, disbelieving but transfixed. I'd seen that look a lot around Bedford Falls. "Mister, you're nuts," she said. "Honest to god, around the bend, never to come home again nuts." She laughed. It was a full-bodied woman's laugh, long and curving as her thigh, and not a nervous thing about it.

"Keep talking, Miss Bick. Let's see what the police say."

"Yeah," she said. "I'd like that too. I'll call them right now. I'll tell them how you've followed me and badgered me all over town. You'll be real popular, mister. They'd love to hear how you busted into my apartment one night and wouldn't leave." She took a swig. "I know that nice Mr. Callaghan would listen. Get lost, mister. I got more business here than you any day."

"That wouldn't surprise me."

Her left hand chipped at the air. Her top feathers were in a frenzy. I got up.

"Tell your friend I've gone home," I said. "He knows the address. I'll be waiting in my car outside. I wouldn't want to drag Mrs. Parker into any more of this. And this time I'm ready for him."

CHAPTER THIRTY-SEVEN

I figured I'd give him until eleven thirty. It was already twenty past. The streetlight cast a circle of cold white light about thirty yards ahead of me, like a spotlight waiting for the star entrance. I rubbed the back of my head a few times. It was still sore. I listened to some melted snow drip through the leak in my car. I was cold and I wanted sleep. I lit a cigarette and filled my lungs with smoke. I took a couple of swigs and waited. The minutes trickled by. I looked at my watch again. Then I looked up.

A light colored sedan was heading towards me. It slowed on the small curve in the road and lowered its lights. I straightened up. I felt for my gun. I was ready. The car was going past me. From what I could see it was more sand colored than gray. The driver wore a woman's hat with a flower on its brim. Once it was past me, the car sped up. Its tail lights glowed red in the cold night, and then disappeared. I yawned and took another swig. I looked around at the tall hedges and the shadows. I felt as though I were being watched by stealthy animals with cruel yellowish eyes.

It was eleven-thirty. I could be waiting here all night with nothing to show for it but a hangover. That's if I were lucky. I needed to tell the Baileys what I knew before something happened to me - something named Nick, or Clement, whichever he preferred. But I needed sleep even more. I dragged myself out of the car and went to bed.

The next morning was gray and clear. Light shone blearily through the window. I heard a car pass by on the road, and a truck, and that was all. Then I remembered today was Saturday. I blinked, and got up. My head was in pretty good shape. I wouldn't put in for a new one after all. I was washed, shaved, and dressed before nine. I opened the front door.

"Up at the crack of dawn, eh?" Mrs. Parker' cackled from upstairs. I got in my car and headed over to 320 Sycamore. No one followed me. I parked in front, walked up the steps, and knocked on the door. The snowman was a snow midget but still standing. I waited. Maybe folks like the Baileys didn't answer their door before ten o'clock, on a weekend. I wasn't sure. I didn't have much experience with folks like the Baileys.

"Yes? Who is it?" a man's voice said through the door.

"It's me. Incles. I need to talk with Mary Bailey. Right away. It can't wait."

The door opened. Harry Bailey stood there. He didn't look right just standing there. He should have been swaggering, or chewing gum, or arguing about something he knew nothing about. He had grey shadows under his eyes, as though the blood had gotten tired of reaching so remote an area. He looked at me, and stepped aside.

"What's the big idea?" he said.

"The case just cracked wide open."

Harry blinked. Maybe my brilliance was too dazzling that early in the morning. Then he gave me a tired grin. It took its time making it across his face and it didn't stay long. "That so? I wondered when we'd be hearing from you, pal." He crossed his arms. "Mary's tending to the kids. I'll get her. Come on in." I already had.

Mrs. Hatch was sitting on the sofa. She had a faraway

look in her eyes as if she was trying to remember something.

"You'll be okay, for a moment, ma'am?" Harry said.

She nodded without looking at him. Probably Harry had said something stupid again, or waved his medals around one time too many.

"I'll be right back." Harry frowned and hurried upstairs.

"Hello, Mrs. Hatch." I sat down.

She turned and looked at me as though she had never seen me before.

"It looks like Mr. Bailey will be a free man soon," I said. "The case is pretty much cracked."

She was still looking at me. She didn't blink. Then she spoke. "Young man, do you have the time?" Her voice was toneless and flat, about as fit to carry conversation as a disconnected phone line.

I looked at my watch. "Ten past nine."

Her chin started nodding up and down mechanically, in little spasms, like a toy dog that needed a new battery. "Ten past nine. My Marty was still alive at ten past nine," she said. "On a morning just like this. All alone on a big battlefield. They say he didn't suffer. Not a bit." Then her back started rocking too, faster and faster. She looked right through me to the front yard.

Harry came into the room. Mrs. Bailey hurried after him.

"Mr. Incles, I understand you've got everything straightened out," she said. "This calls for a celebration!"

Mrs. Bailey sat down next to Mrs. Hatch, who had quit warbling and was just nodding her chin. Harry took the chair across from me. He leaned forward, stuck his feet out, and put his face in his hands.

"It all fits together now," I said. "I suppose I should have figured it from that sedan. Someone's been following me the past few days."

Mrs. Bailey's right hand flew to her face. "Oh, my!"

"That's the business I'm in, Mrs. Bailey," I said. "It's not the life for everyone. My line of work means I walk a lonely mile. I lie awake through the desperate hours. And even when I do sleep, it's with my eyes wide open." Harry shifted his feet around. I went on. "No, it's not an easy life, Mrs. Bailey. Someone also hit me over the head last night. Someone who was afraid of what I knew. Someone who was guilty. I had some help, of - "

"Of course, with a heart as weak as Marty's, they had no business sending him," Mrs. Hatch said. Her toneless voice cut into mine like the prow of a battleship, steely and dull. "I'll have to talk to Mr. Potter again. Get him to change his mind. Mr. Potter will listen this time. I'll make him."

Mrs. Bailey turned to her mother. She was worried and embarrassed, so I went on. "A friend in Albany had a tip for me, and it panned out."

Harry jerked his face up. "Albany? A tip? Let's just cut to the chase, mister."

"Twelve past nine," Mrs. Hatch said. "My Marty."

Harry put his face back in his hands.

"As I was saying, my friend looked a few things up, and maybe I should have figured it all out right then." I took out a cigarette. "But it took me a little time." Something was beginning to nag at me. Marty on a battlefield, in the morning. Twelve past nine.

Twelve past nine. That was the time on the pocket watch, the one with large "G" engraved on it. G was for George, alright: for George Hatch, Marty's father. I remembered the confusion the first time I spoke to Mrs. Hatch. Marty Hatch had fallen dead. His father's watch had fallen with him, and been left by the pool the night Whittier was killed.

I put the cigarette back and rummaged in my pocket for the watch.

Harry stood up. His face was white as a baked cod on a snowy night. He tried a short laugh. It faltered at about knee-height and fell over. "What's the matter, Incles?" he said. "You got ants in your pants or something?"

"No, Harry, I don't. And it looks like I don't have a pocket watch either."

He caught my eye for a second too long. I knew what had happened. And he knew I knew. It was all over.

CHAPTER THIRTY-EIGHT

"Mrs. Hatch, Mary, excuse us a minute," Harry said.

"I don't understand - " Mrs. Bailey began. She stood up.

"It's my car, Mrs. Bailey," I said. "Harry's afraid if it sits in the cold much longer, it'll never start. You understand."

"Well, no," she said.

"Don't worry, Mary," Harry said. "We'll be right back."

She kept looking out the window as Harry and I got into my car. I drove off.

"Where to?" I said.

"Doesn't matter." He edged as far as he could towards the car door.

"You'll be pleased to know I'm healing nicely, Harry. The bruise has shrunk and now it's hardly any bigger than the back of my head. Of course, you didn't know I got hurt, did you? Sapped on the back of the head outside Mrs. Parker's last night. Before that, I'd been followed. But I already told you this."

"Okay, Mr. Incles. You've made your point."

I drove a few blocks and then pulled over by the side of the road. It was as quiet a street as you'd find in Bedford Falls. A few kids up ahead were having a snowball fight.

"Let's just sit here," I said. "It's a nice neutral spot. You tell me the story straight. Save us both a lot of running around, and your brother from making a trip to the chair."

"I guess you figured out most of it by now," Harry said. "Potter was in charge of the board that drafted Marty - and Mrs. Hatch is right, there's no way Marty was fit to serve. Couldn't even play stickball with the rest of us kids. We used to laugh at him, sitting on the sidelines. More shame on us." Harry looked down at his hands a moment and then straight ahead into the road. "Marty's death hit her pretty hard. And then all this with George, and Potter fixing to ruin her daughter's life too. It was all too much for her. I don't think even she knows exactly why she went over there. Maybe to scare Potter, to get him to leave George and Mary alone. It's hard to get any kind of sense out of her." Harry turned and looked at me. "She went over there armed with Marty's watch – the only thing she had left of him, and her husband's old service revolver. She saw Potter sitting there, in front of all that money, and she knew what Potter had been up to. That pile of cash -"

"The eight thousand dollars from the Building and Loan," I said.

Harry nodded. "Money was the only thing Potter ever loved. So Mrs. Hatch ordered him to eat it. At gunpoint. I can't say I wouldn't have done the same. And then... Well, maybe he choked, maybe he had a heart attack. It doesn't really matter, does it." He looked at me. "But she didn't mean to kill him. I know that for a fact, Mr. Incles. She must have been in a panic when she dropped Marty's watch. And she didn't know Potter was dying until it was too late."

A golden spaniel struggled over the top of a snow bank. We watched the dog for a moment and then Harry went on. "Whittier found the watch in Potter's office. And put two and two together, and came up with a way to get a few thousand. Blackmail."

That all fit. "Whittier said Potter's death was a bigger bonanza than he'd ever hoped," I said. "He thought Mrs. Hatch was going to be his windfall. Then he found out he was in line for a much bigger one, thanks to Potter's will." I took out a cigarette and lit it. I took a long slow drag. "Is that why she met him by the pool those times? Was Whittier collecting his payments?"

Harry nodded. "All but the last time. I think he was through blackmailing her. It wasn't worth his while anymore, once he knew about the will. My guess is he brought Marty's watch because he wanted to give it back to her. Maybe he was even grateful to her, for Potter's death." He laughed. "Funny, isn't it. Whittier was about to end the thing, only Mrs. Hatch went and ended Whittier. Of course, Whittier was the one who'd let her into Potter's office Christmas Eve."

That would make it just after I'd left Potter's, around eleven-thirty. Whittier left Potter's office, and went over to Callaghan, to dish dirt on Potter since Potter was putting a squeeze on Violet Bick. That was when he had no idea he was in Potter's will. The stuff in the file, the bad bank loans, they were all suckers Potter had in mind to bleed. Potter knew who Nick was, and would have starting putting the squeeze on him. But Potter got whacked instead. Whittier never knew about Nick. He had his own sucker, Mrs. Hatch. Probably he heard Mrs. Hatch and Potter arguing as he left. He knew she hated Potter, and why. When he returned with Callaghan and found Potter dead, it didn't take a genius to figure the angles. He'd flexed his waxy yellow fingers and flinched the watch from right under Callaghan's pale blue eyes.

"Mrs. Hatch ran across the watch this morning," Harry went on. "Found it my sock drawer when she was putting away the laundry. That damn watch. She'd been pretty tough up to then, but when she saw it, she fell apart."

A snowball thudded against the left rear window. A kid staggered through the snow up ahead and dived behind a garbage can.

"She's dropped plenty, in bits and pieces," Harry went on. "Especially about the night Whittier died. She waited for him at the gym. She stationed herself at the far end. Then she got the idea that she could keep him from getting to her this time. She set the pool timer running. Whittier came in and started coming towards her. He was saying something like it was all over and his voice echoed around the gym. He didn't notice the floor was moving apart until it was too late. He lost his balance and fell in. Hit his head along the way." He looked out the window. "At least that's the best she can remember." He turned to me. "You believe her?"

"It fits," I said. "You know that I have to go to the police with this." The kids up ahead were screaming like a nest of eagles.

"With what? You don't even have the watch."

"You saw to that," I said.

"And you won't have my testimony either. Not a word, brother."

I blew some smoke out of my mouth, slow and easy, and looked at him.

"Just leave town," Harry said. "George may be the suspect the police have the most evidence against, but it's still not much. Just a bag of hunches and maybes and coincidences. There's nothing to it."

"You think you can risk your brother George?"

"As opposed to sacrificing Mary's mother? Yes, I do." His chin reasserted itself. "And that's what George wants too."

"Does Mary know?" I said.

"Not from me she doesn't. She knows her mother's a bit peculiar, but she chalks it up to Marty's death, and worrying about George. That's all I've let on."

"Fair enough. If anything's fair in this mixed up town."

But I knew I still had to talk to George Bailey. It was his call.

CHAPTER THIRTY-NINE

Callaghan had the day off. The fresh-faced kid with wrists like pencils was on duty. He was reading another comic book.

"What's Callaghan up to?" I said. "Catching butterflies?"

"Ha," the kid said. He turned back to his comic. "Mr. Bailey's there in back."

I whistled down the hallway. I didn't feel like whistling, but I thought if I whistled, I would. I didn't.

George was lying on his side on the bunk. His mouth was open, as if there were something in front of him that he couldn't believe. He was reading.

"Mr. Bailey?" I said.

George stood up. His lips were white, and his face whiter. He gripped the bars of the cell.

"Harry told me all about Mrs. Hatch," I said. "And what you've decided to do."

George Bailey looked at me dead level. His eyes weren't crazy anymore. And he wasn't surprised, not a bit.

"Mr. Bailey, I was hired to clear you. I can't allow you to face charges for crimes I know you didn't do. Mrs. Hatch could get help. Any judge would see she wasn't in

165

control of herself when she went and - "

"Hold on, mister," he said. "Hold on a darned minute! I'm not getting her into this. Mrs. Hatch – it would destroy her! And Mary. And me. They don't have anything on me. And even if they did, well, if one of us has to go to jail for this thing, it's going to be me. That's how I want it. Give me this much, Mr. Incles, man to man."

I had to hand it to him.

"Did you tell your wife anything?"

"Not a thing," he said. "And I never will."

I looked at him and pushed my hat back a few inches. "It's your call, Mr. Bailey. But you should think about it. Callaghan's case may collapse but he won't let it go easy."

"I've thought all I need to," George said. "Thanks for all your help, Mr. Incles." He lay down flat on his bunk, and stared at the ceiling, straight into the light bulb. Then he reached for the book beside him, opened it, and put it over his eyes.

Like I said, it was his call.

CHAPTER FORTY

The train station was on the other side of town. On the platform, a few travellers were waiting. Some paced up and down in the cold dry air, and others sat bundled up and immobile on the benches.

I went to the ticket booth. The ticket seller was slight and balding. The end of his nose was kept in check by a pair of gold-rimmed specs that gripped him like a clothespin. Maybe that explained the voice.

"Help you?"

"A ticket to Los Angeles," I said. "One way."

"Long trip," he said, as he made out the ticket.

"It been busy today?" I said.

"Nope. Not with all that snow that's been on the tracks. When it gets wet, it's the worst, heavy as stone to move. Not a blessed train went out yesterday, or even this morning. Good thing folks don't want to travel much in this weather anyway. But it's getting back on track. Yours shouldn't be delayed. Leaves in three hours, the last one out that way. Mind your transfers. Wouldn't mind going with you though. California. I bet it's eighty degrees and the sun is shining. You been that way before?"

"Only in my dreams," I said.

He smiled. "Here you go." I took the ticket and paid him. I went to the platform and sat down.

A man and a woman with a small white dog went up to the ticket booth together. The dog sniffed eagerly at the man's trouser cuff, and the man gave him a small kick. A smartly-dressed brunette walked back and forth along the platform, smoking. She threw the cigarette butt to the platform and ground it into the concrete with her high-heeled shoe. She had the warm and friendly expression of a dame who breaks wedding engagements long-distance.

A broad-shouldered, dark-haired man sidled onto the platform. He kept his head down, but that didn't make him any smaller. The little white dog ran away from the woman, trailing its leash. It ran towards the man, jumped up on him, and ran around him in a circle.

"Peaches!" the woman called. "Get back here!"

The man looked up. I'd recognize that scowl anywhere. The reason I was at the station had just pulled in.

CHAPTER FORTY-ONE

"Leaving town, Nick?" I said. "That's a new one."

"What about it? It's a free country."

"But not for everybody. Not for fraudsters. Not for Clement Walters, who ran a bad checks scheme and skipped out of the Charles Street jail. Maybe you've heard of him."

He took in enough breath so that when he expelled it, it would be felt as a gentle breeze in Bermuda. His jaw looked sullen and set in granite. "I thought you knew too much," he said.

"You tried clearing out of town last night, but the trains weren't running."

He looked at me. "Yeah? What are going to do about it?"

"I'm going to send you away. To Los Angeles. I have the ticket. And I'm going to give you plenty of lead time before I give the police your confession."

"My confession?" he said.

"The one you're about to write. The one in which you admit to killing Henry Potter, and then Charles Whittier. Because each in turn knew who you were, and began blackmailing you. You got angry and maybe you didn't know your own strength."

"And if I don't?"

"There's a nice policeman in front of the station."

"Yeah?"

"He'll want to have a long chat with you after I tell him the whole story."

Nick's chin stayed square but the light in his eyes faltered.

"I even have a picture of you," I said. "Ran in the papers. Clement is a very nice name."

"Hold it there, mister. Murder's a big rap. I don't like it."

"But you'd like coming with me now and going into the slammer for fifteen years, minimum, a whole lot less. This is as close to a clean break as you'll ever get."

He looked hard at the horizon. It didn't budge. Then he tried me. I didn't either. "Okay, Incles. You win."

"I think I can guess, but where were you headed?"

"Boston. The only dame I've ever wanted is Velma. And someday I thought I'd go looking for her. Only you got hold of me."

"I get the feeling that now you're headed in the right direction, bub," I said. "The city of the angels is the only place for a woman like Velma."

He nodded.

*

It was a nice farewell. I had his letter tucked inside my coat. I watched him get on the train and rattle off into oblivion. I would deliver the letter to Callaghan, on Sunday night, along with the photograph. For a cop like Callaghan, the pieces were all there. Nick had motives and opportunity, and more than that, he was a hot-tempered ex-con on the run. And now he'd skipped town. If Callaghan worked overtime to smarten up, he'd buy it, and it would stick. I'd done my best to make sure he'd never find Nick. If the police even traced Nick to the station, the ticket seller would remember selling him a ticket to Boston, and the chase would run off in the wrong direction. So the case would remain in its simplest form.

CHAPTER FORTY-TWO

"Pretty funny Nick left you the confession, isn't it?" Callaghan said. It was eleven o'clock, New Year's Eve. His eyes were unconvinced and icy. They meant business. But his thin, bloodless lips curved downwards in a frown like a fallen arch in an old shoe. The bottom two-thirds of his face was ready to call the case closed.

"He knew what I had on him," I said.

"But why confess? Why not just skip town?"

"It's a funny thing about crooks, Callaghan. They cheat and they steal. When they're cornered and they figure they have to, they even kill. But in some ways, they're more honest than most other people. It's not Nick's style to leave someone else hanging for his two drops when the game is over for him anyway."

Callaghan snickered.

"Don't get me wrong," I said. "I'm not saying Nick is a decent fellow or even a half-nice guy or anything like that. But he's an old fashioned crook. The kind who in the end skipped out of jail rather than rat and let the cops set him free. In a way, that's what he's doing now, in his terms. He'd be ratting on George Bailey if he didn't say something." I took out a cigarette. "Anyway, that's how I figure it."

"How original. A thief's honor," Callaghan said. "Can it, mister." He turned back to the papers on his desk.

"I guess this is adios," I said.

He didn't look up. I could have almost felt sorry for him, if I were a compassionate sort. But I wasn't and I didn't. I felt hungry. I headed over to Martini's and had the dinner special and a scotch. I remembered there was something else I needed to settle.

320 Sycamore was lit up like a ferris wheel, just like the first time I'd seen it. The door was wide open and I went in. The room was packed with people, and full of music and laughter. One of the brats was plunking out a one-fingered tune on the piano. Mr. Gower stood beside it, dapper and sober, leading a small group in song. Ernie was by the staircase, telling Uncle Billy and the man from the newspaper some long involved joke. Uncle Billy didn't get it and Ernie had to go over it again. Then they were all laughing. Violet Bick was standing by the sideboard, under a silver-lettered banner that read "Happy New Year." She was dressed in midnight blue. In the center of the room were George and Mary Bailey. They were laughing too.

"Home and free, in time for New Year's Eve. Isn't it wonderful!" George said. His grin was getting wider than his face. He did a double take when he saw me. "And here's the man who did it all - Mr. Incles!"

"Mr. Incles," Harry said. He flashed his pearly whites. He was chewing gum. "Didn't expect to see you again."

"George," I said. "I'm glad to see you're home." I lowered my voice. "There's a certain matter of money."

His smile fell. You could almost hear it hit the floor and roll behind the leg of a coffee table like a silver dollar. "That was last week's line, wasn't it? You're not going to pin that one on me again." His eyes glittered like broken glass.

I lowered my voice. I hoped he wasn't going nutsy again. "I mean payment for services rendered."

"Of course you do, Mr. Incles. I was just joking with you," George said. "Isn't this wonderful! Let me just get my checkbook out and - "

Mrs. Bailey grasped hold of his elbow. "We're all still a bit dazed, Mr. Incles. Happy New Year to you."

"Name your price," he said.

"Fifty-five dollars should cover it."

"Fifty-fi-! Mr. Incles, you are an angel," George said. He turned back to the check. "How do I make this out exactly?"

"Richard C. Incles," I said. "I-N-C-L-E-S."

"What's the C for?" George said.

"Do you have to know?"

"Just curious."

"Clarence," I said.

"Clarence?" George said. He stopped writing. He drew his face up to mine and peered into my eyes. "Really?" His voice went kind of soppy and serious, as if I were a long lost buddy. "Did you get your wings, Clarence?"

Once a nut case, always a nut case. I took the check. "Thank you, Mr. Bailey. Mrs. Bailey."

Martini rushed in, a bottle of wine in each hand. Bert followed him. He had an accordion around his neck.

"Sorry I'm late, folks, but traffic detail is something awful tonight." Bert looked at the clock. "Everybody, it's almost time."

The room went quiet. The clock stirred and struck midnight. Then they all cheered, and burst into Auld Lang Syne. I took a cup of kindness on my way out. Violet Bick followed me onto the front steps. I stopped and listened to the singing.

"Hey, soldier," she said.

"Why aren't you in there, Miss Bick?"

"Money," she said. "You'll want your money."

"Money," I said. I snorted. "Sure. My payoff for keeping mum about your tax problem. Because money's all I ever think about. That's why I'm in this business. I'm devoured by greed. That's why I get hauled in by the police, twice, and sapped on the back of the head. I get chewed out by college boys, I dodge rock-faced ex-cons, and I risk my future, and the hatred of the cops and the entire DA's office. I do all this for twenty-five dollars a day plus expenses - and maybe just a little bit so that nice woman in there can go to bed knowing that her husband, while he might be nutty or a bit soft in the head, is no murderer. That whatever corruption it is that lines this town like a sewer doesn't touch them, at least not now, or yet. You think I'm a son of gun, don't you? Well, I've been called a lot worse by a lot tougher numbers. So how much are you offering me, Miss Bick, and why? If I take it, do I go on being a son of a gun, or do I get to become a gent, like that yellow-faced goon you had on the bean for so long?"

Her eyes were blank disks. She blinked, and held something out to me. "Your check," she said. "You dropped it on your way out."

I took the check, folded it, and put in my wallet. "Thank you Miss Bick. Now why don't you go back in there and sing? Should old acquaintance and all that?"

"There's a new acquaintance I'd like to make," she said. Her voice was soft as velvet, but husky, as though there was something that had been caged up inside her for a long time and needed to get out. Her eyes looked up at me. She was lovely enough in the light, but even more lovely in the dark. "And maybe make him more than an acquaintance. His name is Richard Incles, and I'd like him to kiss me."

The singing from the Bailey house filled the steps. They were on the second chorus. Far in the cold distance, a train horn sounded. It was a clear night. A shooting star cut across the sky. One of Bailey brats, the kid with the crazy name and the pocket watch, came to the window and stared at us. I looked out over Bedford Falls and its twisted streets.

I looked at Violet Bick. Auld Lang Syne thundered on. She nodded. We wandered off together down the dark and lonely street. The train whistled again into the night. It reminded me of Nick, and Clement Walters, but I never heard of either one of them again.